THE STEEL NOOSE

by Arnold Drake

Black Gat Books • Eureka California

THE STEEL NOOSE

Published by Black Gat Books
A division of Stark House Press
1315 H Street
Eureka, CA 95501, USA
griffinskye3@sbcglobal.net
www.starkhousepress.com

ISBN: 979-8-88601-092-3

Cover design by Jeff Vorzimmer, ¡caliente!design, Austin, Texas
Book design by Mark Shepard, shepgraphics.com
Proofreading by Bill Kelly

First Stark House Press/Black Gat Edition: April 2024

THE STEEL NOOSE

"Mystery novel from an award winning icon in the comic book world. Drake created The Doom Patrol and Stanley and His Monster. He also wrote a lot for Little Lulu Comics as well as Star Trek and Twilight Zone Comics along with many others... a good, tough crime novel and worth picking up."—*Vintage45's Blog*

"As far as I know, THE STEEL NOOSE is Arnold Drake's only novel. That's kind of a shame because it's really good and he might have given us more like it... I give it a high recommendation."—James Reasoner, *Rough Edges*

"*The Steel Noose* is a fine, hardboiled crime novel. Loaded with clever patter, elements of noir, and a cocky protagonist who manages to right himself after several missteps along the way—some nearly fatal. All-in-all, a terrific read."—Richard Krauss, Larque Press

"A satisfyingly twisty tale loaded with betrayal, venality, obsession, violence, murder and crazy love."—Paul Burke, *CrimeTime*

To
PEARL and LILY
My jewel and my flower

CHAPTER ONE

I was quietly paring my nails at a table for two in the Flamingo Club. It was a Monday night. Nothing happens at the Flamingo on Mondays. That's why I always bring a good nail parer with me. For that reason and because I know Charlie Weaver doesn't like people to pare their nails at the Flamingo on any night. He also doesn't like people who wear polka dot ties with striped suits. That's how I got run out of the Flamingo the first time.

But that's neither here nor in Chicago. The fact is that Charlie doesn't hate me anymore. As a matter of fact he practically loves me ever since I got myself a byline on the *Morning Express*. Now I can walk into the Flamingo without a tie—or anything else, for that matter. That's the power of the press for you.

As I said, I was sitting quietly at this table for two, hoping that Milton Berle might walk in to tell me an old joke or Arthur Godfrey might come by to run his hand through my hair and call me "Sonny." I needed one more item to close my column for the night and it didn't look like I was going to get it. Then in walked "Ears" Murdock.

Let me explain how I happen to know Ears. Back around 1935, after Roosevelt had called an end to prohibition, a lot of the racket boys hung on to their speakeasies and tried to turn into legitimate bars and nightclubs. One of these was a joint on 52nd Street owned by a New York mob. I did a tap dance routine there for a couple of weeks, told a few jokes, sang a song or two. I thought I was the greatest thing since

Jolson. I was terrible.

One night one of the mob boys got real drunk and started shooting slugs at my feet while I was out dancing. I beat it off the floor and never went back. The next day I got a job on the *Morning Express* and began eating regularly. I've been grateful to Ears Murdock ever since. He's the guy who shot me out of show business.

Ears walked into the Flamingo that night wearing a dinner jacket that fit him like the skin fits a banana. There was no pistol bulge to mar the hundred-dollar lines of the jacket. And only a few old friends called him "Ears" now. Murdock was fifteen years a legitimate business man.

"I got news," Murdock said. He took a deep breath and his ears wiggled. They'd been doing that ever since he got his face creased by a slug years before and a few muscles became scrambled. "Jimmy Maranville is getting married. A blonde model from Ohio. Good looker."

I smiled. Maranville was a sixty-year-old nitrate king whom the headline writers still called "Playboy." He had been married eleven times. "Jimmy Maranville getting married isn't news," I said. "It's a daily feature, like the comic strips." But I made a quick note in my little black book.

"That's all I've got, Boyd," he said.

"That and money," I said.

He laughed and patted me on the back. "You don't need money, Boyd. You've got principles." He walked away.

"Hey," I called after him, "I'll trade you."

The Maranville item wasn't a big deal but I didn't need a big deal to close my column. I could have stuck in a filler, an old joke made new by crediting it to some Broadway name. I could even have stuck in one of those blind items that columnists create to fill space and start people talking: "What underwear model has what international Yo-Yo champion whirling?" But the Maranville item was better than either. So I put my nail file away, tipped the waiter, pinched the hat check girl and left.

My car was in a parking lot nearby. I got in and drove down to Greenwich Village. I like the Village. It's where I live, where I eat veal and chicken, Italian style, and guzzle Scotch and Chianti. But my readers pay for the Chianti so I write what they want—the Flamingo Club, El Morocco, etc.

I left my car outside the garage, which is about four blocks from my house, and decided to walk home. Generally the garage man drives me back. But there was a hard, cold April rain falling so I walked. If Congress were to pass a law against starvation I'd probably stop eating just to prove something. You might say I'm obstinate.

I tried being hard-working and cooperative for the first twenty-five years of my life and I never made a dime. So I became an obstinate bum for the last fifteen years and I've never wanted for gold silk bathrobes and thirty-dollar shoes.

I passed Club 41 along the way and decided to drop in for a nightcap. Generally I stay away from bars and clubs when I'm not working. But 41 is a different story. The place is so cruddy, so patently phony that I find I can relax there.

Outside Club 41 rain was falling in buckets the way it always does in New York in April. Inside was noisy, smoky and slightly polluted, the way it always is at

Club 41. The pollution comes mostly from the queers and lesbians who make 41 their headquarters. The rest of the pollution comes from the rich thrill-seekers who go slumming in the Village to watch men acting like women and vice-versa.

I stood at the bar watching the show. Two fags were trying to pick up a sailor.... A lesbian, a short stocky dame in a leather jacket and slacks, was yelling at some guy for making a pass at her girlfriend. The girlfriend giggled through it all. She liked being fought over.... A kid, maybe seventeen or eighteen, was buying beers for a painted doll who looked like his mother's older sister.... A fine, wholesome atmosphere.

There's a jazz trio—piano, bass and sax—that plays at Club 41. The piano man is a tall, serious-looking Negro who plays Gershwin and Rodgers like they were Bach and Beethoven. He can probably play that stuff too, but that's not what he gets paid to do.... I looked over in the direction of the musicians and past them to a dark corner where I saw a familiar face. One arm that came with the face waved at me.

"Hi, Boyd, old man," he called.

If I hadn't recognized the face I'd have known the voice. It was Calvin Stockton. To Calvin everybody is either "old man" or "old boy." He was sitting at a small table with a redheaded dame who looked twice as knocked out as anything the trio was playing. I got up and started for their table. Stockton was news, which is my racket. The redhead was a pleasure, which is my hobby. I decided to mix a little of each.

Calvin was part of the younger generation of New York's social register, Harvard Law School, Class of '42, Air Force Captain, Class of '43-'45, junior partner in the firm of Stockton, Stockton, Himmelholt and

Stockton. Born with a silver spoon in his mouth and two nurses to hold it there.

"Good to see you, old man," Calvin said. He shot out a long bony hand from under the cuff of his ten-dollar shirt and got a steely grip on mine. I squeezed back twice as hard just to let him know that the gang from Public School 179 was ready to take on the Harvard crowd on any clear day in Central Park.

"What's such a big deal?" I asked. "I live in the Village."

Calvin raised his eyebrows and gave out with a bluff laugh. "Imagine that," he cried, "living in the Village."

"Lots of people do, you know, Calvin," the redhead purred. That's when I made up my mind to like her. She had the lean, high-cheekbone look that the one buck fashion wags go for. The soft red hair was cut close in back and trimmed in short bangs along the forehead. But the first thing any man would notice about her were her lips. They were full and glistening like ripe red berries almost bursting their skin. You might start by kissing those lips but you'd end up biting them.

"Have a seat, McGee fellow," Calvin said, and he motioned the waiter to slide a chair under me.

I lit a cigarette and sat down. "What brings you down to poor man's country, Calvin?"

"Fabulous place," Calvin bubbled. "You can't imagine the things that go on here."

"I can imagine," I said. "In fact, anything that I can imagine goes on here."

"You must have a vivid imagination," the redhead said.

"Boyd McGee," Calvin said, introducing me. "He has that 'Boyd's Nest' column in the *Express*. And this is

Maura Page, McGee." I nodded. She smiled back at me.

"I've read your column," she said.

"So you're the one," I said. Calvin got a big kick out of that. Then he hunched over the table in my direction and gave me a sly wink.

"I've got a great story for that column of yours only—"

"Only what?" I asked. He shrugged.

Maura pouted. "You can't do that to the man. That's like holding a T-bone steak out to a dog and then muzzling him."

"Thanks for the compliment," I laughed. "Only it's not that way, Calvin. If you've got a hot story that can't be printed I'm still interested. My column is like an iceberg; it only exposes twenty per cent of what I know. The rest is below the water mark, where I can't be sued."

Calvin wasn't convinced. I flicked some ashes into a tray and looked him square in his baby blues.

"Like the Seaview Trust Company operation," I said. He blinked twice. "I'd be the last to shoot my mouth off about the stock transfer deal your firm swung for Seaview last year. Of course I know that some of the newer stockholders took a three-to-one whipping on it and only some fast money hushed the whole—"

"McGee!" Calvin cautioned. "You realize the Seaview transfer was totally legal."

"Naturally," I said, and I knew damn well it was. Stockton, Stockton, Himmelholt and Stockton wouldn't be caught transacting anything but a legal deal. It's all a matter of your definition of the word "legal." The three Stocktons and lonely Mr. Himmelholt had cash assets to back up their definition, which is more than you can say for the dictionary.

"Oh, come on," Maura said. "Tell him about it, Calvin." He motioned to the waiter for another round of drinks.

"Of course you understand that this must be kept in the strictest—uh—" He ran his hand across the top of his scrubby head. At thirty-four Calvin still affected the college boy haircut. "Not that I don't trust you, McGee fellow, but it would be well if I told you this without names."

The drinks came and Calvin polished his off with a flick of the ten-dollar cuff. He wiped his mouth with a crisp linen handkerchief. "It concerns a client of Stockton, Stockton, Himmelholt and Stockton, a man we'll call—Smith."

"That's a good one," I said. Maura smiled. Calvin didn't get it.

"Now this Smith, a wealthy enough fellow, is being sued for divorce by a scheming female."

"His wife," I said brightly.

"Naturally," Calvin replied. "His wife is in Reno at present, establishing legal residence. She is suing for one million dollars." I whistled. Calvin laughed. "She won't get a cent, old man."

"You're fighting it?"

"Not at all. Our client is delighted at the prospect of losing her. In addition to which we're not divorce attorneys." Calvin ordered another drink. I sighed.

"Calvin," I said quietly, "would you mind giving me the *Reader's Digest* version? I've still got work to do tonight." He nodded over his new drink and then belted it down, one pinky pointed high in the air. He was one of the most dignified lushes in town.

"Mr. Smith's wife is suing for a million but, you see, in a week Smith won't have a nickel to his name. Or,

I should say, in his name." He snickered. I got it now and it was pretty good.

"Let me tell it," I said. "You put a corporation together on paper, all legal and everything. Then you transfer Smith's holdings and cash to the corporation, leaving him flat as a bride's first cake. Except—" I said, and took a sip of scotch.

"Except," he chortled, "Smith happens to have been elected president of said corporation. But you can't sue a corporation for alimony. Technically, Smith is practically bankrupt. Actually he's as rotten rich as ever. With any luck at all we—"

"Luck?" I asked. The way Calvin shaped it everything seemed in the bag.

Maura smiled and took a cigarette from my pack on the table. Calvin and I flicked cigarette lighters simultaneously but she preferred mine. Smiling gray eyes smiled at me over the flame.

"That's the part Calvin doesn't like to talk about, do you, Calvin?" He snapped the lighter shut and said nothing. "You see, there's a race going on between Calvin and Mrs. Smith's attorney. A little race for a million dollars." She leaned back and wafted a thin line of smoke at Calvin. He scowled.

"What about that?" I asked.

"I've done all I can," Calvin said. "The corporation papers are filed and we're waiting for the final okay. That will take ten days to two weeks at the outside."

"And Mrs. Smith's divorce?" I asked. Maura flicked her cigarette at the floor.

"Her legal residence is complete in four days. After that—" She shrugged.

"You're running a losing, race, Calvin," I said.

"Not at all, old fellow. Mrs. Smith's divorce action is

pretty darn weak. Smith has a good divorce attorney, a chap whom Father always recommends in these cases. He should be able to break her case right in two. At best he'll get us a two-week delay. After that it's simply—"

"Suppose he doesn't," I said. "Suppose Mrs. Smith's action goes through without a hitch."

"Those are the chances one takes," Calvin said. "Of course, a wise man is always protected in any eventuality."

He winked at me. It was the broad wink of a guy who is beginning to feel his whiskey.

"Like breaking Mrs. Smith's residence requirement, eh, Calvin?"

"Exactly," Maura said.

"It's an old dodge, but it still works," I said. "They pulled it on Norma Hudson, the producer's wife, just last year. She filed for a Reno divorce and set up her legal residence out there. Hudson wasn't quite ready to fight the case. So he contacted a Hollywood pal who flew up to Reno, took Mrs. Hudson on a drunken date and when she came to they were across the state line. Hudson had three witnesses on hand to testify that she'd been out of Nevada twenty-four hours. That party cost her a quarter of a million."

Calvin shook his head angrily. "Nothing of the sort. S. S. H. and S. would never involve itself in such legal juggling. Of course it was my duty as Ben—uh—Smith's attorney to advise him of all the ramifications." He stumbled over the last word.

"The ins and outs," Maura translated.

"And naturally I explained that it is possible to break a legal residence. But of course the practice is somewhat reprehensible." He stumbled again. Most drunks don't try to handle big words.

"All you gentlemen do," I said, "is load the gun, put it in his hand and aim it for him. Of course if he should just happen to kill somebody—" I shrugged.

"That's rather oversnating—snover—overstating it," Calvin said. And then he burped. It was just a mild burp, as burps go. But for a gentleman such as Calvin it was a clear sign. Calvin was drunk as a skunk.

He put one elbow on the table and rested his head in his hand. "A good attorney must offer his client every assistance this side of legality." His head started to slip and he pulled it back up. "What Smith does with our advice is completely his own affair. But Stockton, Stockton, Himmelholt and Stockton has done its duty." His head skidded off the hand again and he slumped to the table. The last letter of S. S. H. and S. was out like a light.

"Good night, Calvin," Maura said in a bored tone. She'd probably seen friend Calvin do his nose dive a dozen times before.

"Shall we dance?" I asked. She wasn't shocked at the idea.

"Will they let us? They don't permit dancing here."

"Only for friends." I got up and walked down to the small open area where the trio was tootling. Maura followed and climbed into my arms. The Negro piano player gave me a smile and a three-fingered salute with one hand while he kept the slow, soft bass chords rolling with the other.

"Evening, Mr. McGee," he called.

"Evening, Mr. Hoskins," I said.

"You're not a stranger here," Maura murmured. She liked to dance close, real close. If I'd been ten pounds lighter a few parts of her would have gone right through me.

"You carried Calvin home from many of these parties?" I asked.

"A few." She looked up at me and gave me a wicked smile and then she ran her tongue across her lips just a little too deliberately. I figured that Maura Page was either temporarily drunk or permanently oversexed. I pretended not to notice the smile or the tongue and just went on dancing.

"What do you do?" I asked.

"Just live. What else is there?"

"Some work, some let others work for them, some steal," I said.

"I steal," she said. "From my father. He sits behind a big desk in a big office on Wall Street. I let him sit and I steal from him."

"Good racket," I said. She brushed her cheek against mine and slid her hand up behind my neck. We kept on dancing.

"Why did you ask?"

"Just wondered. Friend Calvin is a good catch, if you happen to be hunting. And who isn't?"

"Me. Not for a husband, anyway. There are some who might be hunting me, though." I stopped dancing and took another look at her.

"Maura Page," I murmured. She nodded. I held her chin with one hand and turned her face to one side and then the other. "Faint resemblance, but not quite. The last name's the same and the bank account seems to fit."

"Faint resemblance to what—or whom?" she asked.

"Barbara Page Minton. Sherman Page's daughter. You've heard of the Sherman Pages of Park Avenue, Newport, Miami, the Riviera, etc., etc. The old man is up to his navel in stocks and bonds. A fat old geezer with big ears and a twenty-carat diamond on his pinky." We started dancing again.

"The fat old geezer is my father," she said. We stopped dancing again.

"What are you giving me? Barbara is his daughter."

"He has two," she said. "You're permitted two. But he is fat and kind of old and the diamond is twenty-two carats. Let's dance."

"Where've you been for my past two thousand columns? I thought I knew every rich man's daughter in New York."

"Two years at the University in Mexico and another two at Paris art schools. I've only seen the family on two weekend Miami vacations. They suffocate me." Her hand slid from my neck and tweaked my left ear.

"I understand how they could," I said.

"But I like you," she said. We stopped dancing and I steered her back toward the table.

"Let's pick up Calvin and dump you both in a cab," I said.

"The night is young," she said.

"But I'm not," I said.

We picked up Calvin and between the two of us we got him out to a cab. It had stopped raining and the sky was beginning to clear. A cab spotted us holding up Calvin and made a beeline for us. Cabbies love drunks. Especially the kind that mistake tens for ones.

"Take good care of Calvin," I told her, shoving her in the cab after him.

"Let's let the cabbie take care of Calvin and you take care of me," she said. She climbed out of the cab and gave me a big fat kiss.

"Some other time, honey. I've still got work to do."

"You work and I'll watch. Then later we'll play." Which seemed like a good enough suggestion. Only there was something about the soft, full lips and the narrow, shining gray eyes that looked like trouble. "Okay," I said. "Only I left my cigarettes inside. Wait here, I'll be right out." I ducked back into the club before she could say anything.

"That's a live one you've got there," the piano player said.

"You're telling me!" I walked back into the kitchen, out a rear door and headed for home. I had enough trouble getting out six columns a week without mixing up my life with a nymphomaniac. Particularly a nympho who owned half the world and was out to get the rest.

CHAPTER TWO

New York never sleeps. It might lie down now and then to relax. But it never does more than loosen its tie and maybe take off its shoes. It's no pajamas-and-alarm clock town.

Where else can you walk down a street at three-thirty a.m. and pass a soldier and his girl mushing it up against a lamp post? an all-night fruit stand? two women drunks arguing whether Dempsey could have licked Louis, and three sinister looking characters standing in an alley plotting anything from a newspaper route to mass slaughter?

From Club 41 to my place is six zigzagging blocks, which are the only kind they have in Greenwich Village. The narrow streets are lined with pink and yellow stone houses, crumbling cold-water flats and two-hundred-buck-a-month apartments. Squalor and splendor sit side by side there like friendly enemies.

A familiar cab was parked in front of my house. The cab belonged to Sam Baniff, an ex-mobster turned hackie who ran my stuff over to the paper every morning for a ten-a-week retainer. Sam was also one of the eyes and ears I put out around town to pick up the dirt wherever it falls. For that I paid extra.

Sam's major talents were a good nose for copy and a fine eye for phonies. He would have made a fine newspaperman except for one small matter. When he climbed out of the rackets he forgot to leave some nasty habits behind. He'd never use his brains when he could get what he wanted with a monkey wrench or a roll of dimes packed in his fist. I must have told him a hundred times, "Use your head first, Sam. If that doesn't work, then brain the bastard." But somehow he always got it the other way around.

Sam was studying a racing form by the light of his dashboard when I walked over. I stuck my head in through the open window. "You're early," I said. He jumped a foot and flipped the race sheet under the seat.

"Geez, you scared the livin' skin off'n me," he said.

"Do I smell like a cop? And since when is it against the law to study up on the races?"

"Since cops started hating hackies."

"You've got a persecution complex," I said, and glanced at my watch. "It's a quarter to four. That makes you one hour early. How come?"

"Things was slow uptown. B'sides, I got an item for you and I thought it was hot enough you should want to slip it into tonight's copy."

"Shoot." The column was closed for the night. But

I'd found that when Sam had something to say it was good policy to listen.

He pushed his brown leather cap to the back of his head and leaned across the seat to the open window. "I'm cruising up Madison Avenue somewhere around twelve-twenty tonight. I get a call from this bald-headed guy and his good-looking girlfriend standing outside this plushy apartment house. I'm on the other side of the street so I got to do a U-turn to get to them." He moved one hand through the air to show me how he turned the car.

"So I tool the cab around and scoot up to them, about a second too late. While I'm doing the U some dirty fink of a hackie, an independent cab, comes cowboying up the avenue and tries to steal the fare right out from under my nose. So I tell this pirate just what I think of fare-snatching bastards. Then I turn and give a look at my fare. The guy is just lighting up a cigar and I get a good look at him. It's K. L. Benson."

"So?" I asked.

"You don't get me. I said it was K. L. Benson, the tobacco king." He started singing in a voice that reminded you of chalk being scraped over a slate.

Kingsley Cigarettes are cool
Like a summer dip in a swimming pool.
Kingsley's kind to nose, throat and head.
Keep smoking Kingsley's and you won't drop dead.

"Well, something like that, anyway," he said.

"I know who Kingsley L. Benson is, Sam. But I still ask, who cares? Even a tobacco tycoon has a right to grab the first cab that comes—"

"Who cares!" he gurgled. "This Benson is married.

And the solid-looking broad he's carrying around ain't his wife. Somebody else's, but not his." Sam was baiting a line for me, so I bit.

"All right, lover, whose wife was it?"

"Right off I didn't recognize her. She was wearing her coat collar pulled way up and a floppy hat. But when we pulled away from the streetlamp she lifted her head and I got a good look—Karen Lamain, a dame with two of the best pins that ever kicked in a chorus line. She wasn't a name. The only time she made the papers was when her husband Charlie got run in for trying to knock over a Jersey City bank."

"Charlie Whipper," I grunted.

"Check. Karen married The Whip about a year before he got sent up for the bank job. Only it looks like Karen's getting bored waiting for hubby to serve his time." Sam pulled a cigarette snipe from behind his ear and lit up.

"Makes a good item, Sam. Any time a millionaire starts playing with a gun moll you've got news. But between the two of us, I don't get it."

"You would if you ever saw Karen." He put two fingers and a thumb together, kissed them and then tossed his hand in the air. "Momma!"

"You're sure it was Benson, Sam? Can't afford to slip with a man that big."

"Am I sure I'm Sam Baniff? 'F course it was Benson. He's been in my cab a dozen times. Tall, skinny bozo, hawk nose, shiny scalp, a nervous blink like he should be wearing glasses. That's how sure I am." Like I said, Sam was born with Indian eyes.

I chewed my lower lip awhile. "This Lamain woman was hiding behind a hat, Sam. How come? Did you catch any dialogue from the back seat?"

He smiled crookedly. "They're married. A couple of mice playin' while the cats are away. They got reason to be worried, no?"

I nodded. "It's not the biggest story of the year, Sam, but it's good for a couple of lines in tonight's copy if I can find the room." I pulled my head out of the window and straightened up.

"And how much silver?" Sam asked.

"Fifteen bucks. Put it on the week's bill. See you in fifty-five minutes." Sam went back to the horse sheet, figuring the fastest way to lose his fifteen fish. I scooted up to my Greenwich Village castle, four rooms, a stall shower with a frosted glass door and an electric coffee maker—but I call it home. The landlord calls it a-hundred-eighty-five a month.

I'd been living in the same place for ten years. The last five of those I could have afforded something better, a three-hundred-buck apartment, a ten-grand furnishing job. But where's the percentage? Once you sign a long-term lease on a ritzy four-grand apartment it's not yourself you're working for, it's the landlord.

One of the four rooms at my place was built big enough to stick in your left nostril. Interior decorators say it's a den, but no self-respecting animal would be caught dead in it. There's squeezing space for a desk, filing cabinet, typewriter, shortwave radio and a quart of whiskey. I switched on the desk lamp, turned in the police-call band on the radio and poured myself a double shot. I chucked off my coat and rubbed my hands together to chase some of the April chill from my fingers. It took five minutes to collect the notes I'd made that night and another five to scramble through the files and dig out three items marked for release that date.

Some of the info I pick up hasn't even happened

when I get tipped to it. A guy's getting ready to kick his latest girl out the back door, a producer's planning to sign a new star, a politician is about to pull a coup—all things that are sure to happen. But you can't release that kind of stuff ahead of time or you'll be meeting nothing but closed mouths from Broadway to Washington and back. So I mark a release date on a "hold" item when I get it and, unless I get a call advising me that the deal is off, I shoot it out on schedule.

I took off my shoes, lit a cigarette and poured about half as much whiskey as the first time. The police band was full of wife beatings, second-story jobs and drunk fights. Nothing in it for me. So I lined up my notes and sat down for a hunt-and-peck session with the typewriter. I'd do better with a five-foot-five blonde secretary to type the stuff, but I've never found one who could stand police calls, strong whiskey and the smell of my socks at four in the morning.

By four-thirty I was winding up the column. The last paragraph is a stew pot of names and places around town. That's the grab bag where I chuck in all the miscellanies who've been making the rounds at the Flamingo and 21. That's where I put the item about Jimmy Maranville getting married again, only I held it down to one line to make room for the Kingsley Benson story.

You don't have to do much to make that paragraph, just take out somebody else's wife, drop a bundle in a crap game or get drunk enough to sock a bandleader—the kind of things that any normal, red-blooded moron does on a Saturday night. The difference is that when Reggie Van Swivelgait III does it twenty million readers from Albany to Azuza want to know about it.

I call this particular bundle of nothing "Booze Who." That's where I stuck the item about K. L. Benson.

"Kingsley Benson, the cigarette baron who smokes cigars, was spotted escorting luscious Karen Lamain from her Madison Avenue apartment. Karen's hubby may not get word, he's still serving time across the river. But what about the Madame Benson? Hmmm?"

I read it twice and then decided to tone it down. Sam was positive that he'd made Benson in that cab, but it wasn't worth taking chances with a guy who hires libel lawyers at a hundred G's per year.

I pulled out Benson's name and just used the initials, K.L.B. That was close enough for any nitwit to decipher and cagey enough to save me a lawsuit. If anybody wanted to sue I could always get a hold of somebody named Klaus L. Brinkerhoff, buy him a Bugler cigarette-rolling machine for a half-buck and set him up in business. Then K.L.B. could just as easily be a reference to my own cigarette baron and Benson wouldn't have a legal leg to stamp around on.

I left Karen Lamain's name the way it was. She didn't have any blue-blooded lawyers working for her.

At four-forty I pulled the copy out of the machine, climbed back into my shoes and walked out into the hall. Joe, the elevator man, was standing in the hall waiting. Joe sets his watch by my column. When I stumble out into the hall and hand my copy to him to take it down to Sam waiting at the curb, he knows it's exactly four forty-one. This particular night I didn't give the copy to Joe, I carried it down myself.

The sky seemed lighter already. A milkman down the block was clinking his produce. I turned the copy over to Sam and he gave it the once over while I puffed on a Chesterfield and watched the milkman climb steps. When Sam got to the "Booze Who" items he spotted the cagey reference to Kingsley L. Benson and let out a tch-tch.

"You getting chicken in your old age, Boyd?" I sighed and shot the butt out into the gutter in a bright arc of sparks.

"Sam, I could get sued for a half-million dollar libel but it wouldn't kill the taxi business."

He shrugged it off but he still thought I was chicken. "Keep your eye on the meter," I said, and he hustled his cab off in the direction of the *Morning Express* building.

The milkman clinked back down the stairs. We told each other that it looked like a fine morning for a change. I bought a quart of milk and a box of doughnuts from him. Leaning against his truck, I took long swallows of milk and munched cinnamon doughnuts. An old lady and a cat were pawing through a garbage can down the street.

Two doughnuts and a half quart of milk filled me. I walked down to the old lady, gave her the rest of the doughnuts and spilled out the milk on the sidewalk for the cat. Then I wobbled back up to the apartment and put my Boy Scout head to bed.

I was maybe three minutes into dreamland when the doorbell rang. I pulled the pillow over my head and made like nobody was home. But the doorbell wouldn't go away, so I pushed into some slippers, pulled a bath towel around my midsection and answered it. Lo and get hold, Maura Page, as if I couldn't have guessed.

"That's a cute towel," she said.

"Come back next year," I said.

She ducked under my arm and squeezed through

the doorway. She walked through the foyer into the living room and searched for the light switch. It took her maybe ten seconds. She was good at finding things.

"How'd you get here?" I asked, yawning.

"You're in the phone book, Boyd darling. Getting past the elevator boy was the hard part. He wouldn't even take money."

"Why should he? If he took five from you he'd lose a hundred from me, doll."

She slipped from her coat and walked around the room inspecting the decor. "I finally had to circle the block and scoot up the back. I wouldn't have known about the rear door if a nice old lady munching doughnuts hadn't pointed it out to me."

I nodded. You see, cast you doughnuts on the water and it's sure to wash back a few crumbs.

She finished the inspection tour, walked back into the hall and stood staring at my hairy chest and the towel. "That's nice. New Easter outfit?"

"Scram," I said.

"Where do you keep the scotch?" she asked.

I rubbed an eye with one hand and clutched the towel with the other. "Look, I haven't got a father to steal from. I work. G'night, baby."

She wiggled across the room and up to me. Her arms snaked around my neck. "Let's dance," she said. She started swaying back and forth, rubbing everything she owned against me. I yanked her arms back down.

"Let's not," I said. I walked into the bedroom and slipped on the gold-colored bathrobe. When I came back she whistled.

"You look like a TV wrestler in that thing," she said. "In this corner, ladies and gentlemen, Mister Atom, the fiery, flailing, flamboyant, furious, fighting—" She broke off. "Know any more words that begin with F?"

"A few," I said, quietly as I could. I took a cigarette from the coffee table and lit up. There wouldn't be any more sleep for a while, I knew that.

She plucked the cigarette from between my lips and took a puff on it. When she returned it, I turned and lit another one. She smiled crookedly. "You're not exactly passionately, madly, violently in love with me, are you, McGee?"

"Not exactly," I said.

She sighed. "Ah well, we've only known each other two hours. That sort of thing usually takes three. However, you don't have to be madly, passionately, violently in love with me just to want to—"

I let her have four fingers across the cheek. Just a light, stinging slap. She whimpered. "This is my place, my castle, not a pigsty. You want a quick roll in the hay, go someplace else. Go uptown to the fancy nightclubs. Go float on somebody's yacht. Don't dirty up my place."

"Thanks," she whispered. She put her fingers to the red spot that I had left on her cheek. "I didn't know you were the noble kind. I didn't think anybody who made his living shoveling manure was sensitive about the smell."

"Well, I am," I yelled. "I am," I repeated, this time more softly. "I write what people want to read. But I live the best way I know how."

She smiled crookedly again. "And I'm not exactly the best way you know, eh?" I didn't say anything. She picked up her coat. She had to pass me to get to the door. She stopped along the way.

"Did I ever show you where the horse bit me?" She pulled down the shoulder of her silver evening blouse far enough to show me she wasn't wearing anything underneath. I lowered my head and rubbed the back of my neck. She shrugged and pushed the shoulder back up again. "I live the best I know how, too," she said and started for the door.

She never got past it. Instead she just folded up against the doorframe. There wasn't a sound out of her. It took a while before I understood she was crying, it was that soft.

"Look," I said.

"Shut up," she sobbed. I walked over and put one hand on her shoulder.

"Look, I was tired. I've had a long day. I said the first thing th—"

She turned and threw her head on my shoulder. "I won't go. Don't make me go. I don't want to be alone. Don't send me home."

"But—" This kid was nuttier than I thought.

She pulled her head back and dabbed at her eyes with the back of one hand. "I'll just stay. We won't even talk. You could sleep if you want."

"I intend to," I said.... We settled down on the living room couch. She leaned her head on my shoulder and started talking. I turned out the light. She dozed off in a few minutes. I followed right behind her.

I woke up a while later. My shoulder was numb, I eased her off me and slipped out from under. I made it halfway to the bedroom before she woke up.

"Boyd?" she whispered. "Don't go. Please don't go, Boyd."

So I stretched out on the rug and put one hand up on the couch to let her know I was still there. I slept that way all night. It was no more than you'd have done for a sick dog.

CHAPTER THREE

I stirred once during the night. It seemed that I heard her get up and leave the couch. She rustled around in the darkness and then settled down beside me on the rug. I thought I felt a naked thigh pressed against me. I told myself it was part of a dream....

I don't know how long the phone was ringing, could have been a minute or an hour, before it got through to me.

I opened one eye and a gray, dismal light slanted down at me through the window blinds. The phone was a red-hot needle probing my brain with rhythmic intensity. I rolled my head over to the right and saw the forest-green rug of the living room.

I rolled the other way and saw the smooth, ivory tones of the body of a naked woman. And then it all came back to me: the milkman, the old lady with the doughnuts and swivel tongue, and finally Maura Page. And then I remembered the dream and the naked thigh. Only it wasn't a dream. And the phone went right on ringing.

I crawled as far as the archway and managed to get up and stumble the rest of the way. In the foyer I groped for the phone table, my eyes still half-shut. I found the phone with one swipe and it went clunking to the floor. I collapsed beside it, went flat on my back and picked up the receiver.

"Hello," I said or something like it.

"McGee?" Calvin Stockton was wide awake. "You were a long while answering."

"I was in Shanghai for the weekend," I said. I opened

one eye wide and stared up at the ceiling.

"You are a vile, corrupt and faithless man!"

"I am?"

"You knew the delicate situation that confronted my client—Mr. Smith. How could you stab me in the back this way?"

"Says what?"

"I don't know how you gained his name, but I can guess. And the use you made of it is the most contemptible, unethi—"

"Smith? Smith's name? Calvin, what in hell are you talking about and what time is it?"

"Nine-thirty. It would have been enough if you had merely revealed the information I gave you last night. But—"

"Nine thirty! Calvin, be a good boy and call back at noon." I started groping for the phone base to hang up.

"Wait!" Calvin shrieked. "You deliberately pried the man's name out of Maura and then spread this foul story about some chorus girl being seen with him. That, McGee, was dirty!"

"You've got it all screwed up, Calvin," I sighed. "I didn't pry anything out of Maura. It was the other way around. And the only item about a chorus girl in this morning's column is the one about Karen Lamain and—" Both eyes opened now and the ceiling seemed to fly down at me. "Kingsley Benson!" I hissed.

"I swear, McGee, I could kill you for this. If I don't, Benson will. You knew that Smith was Benson. You can bet your bottom dollar that Mrs. Benson will now switch her divorce grounds to infidelity and name Karen Lamain co-respondent. We can thank you for that, McGee."

"You're welcome," I said. "Look, for what it's worth, Calvin, you've got my word that I didn't know Smith was Benson. It's one of those crazy coincidences. If you want to blame somebody for this go dig up Kingsley L. Benson. Any chump on a divorce hook who hasn't got the brains to keep away from a ton of trouble like Karen Lamain deserves all he gets."

"Don't squirm out of this one, McGee."

I was getting fed up. "I don't squirm, Calvin. Sometimes I stomp and sometimes I trample but I never squirm or crawl. Now get it straight: the Benson item is verified information bought and paid for; Maura Page had nothing to do with it; the information about Smith's stocks and bonds is still top secret and will stay that way till you give me an okay to release it. And finally, I'm going back to sleep now. If this phone rings once more before noon I'm coming down to that velvet office of yours and break your back!"

With those gentle words I dropped the phone back into its cradle and closed my eyes. Then I crawled back into the living room and passed out.

When the phone rang again I woke with a start, both eyes wide open this time. I scrambled up from the floor and grabbed my watch off the end table. It was nine forty-five. I stomped into the foyer and yanked the phone from the cradle.

"Just wait where you are," I snarled. "I'll be down in fifteen minutes and if I don't break your back it won't be because I didn't try."

"That's what I'd like to see you do, Jack," the voice said. "Just try, that's all."

"Calvin?" I asked.

"No. And it ain't Percy or Melvin either." That voice was a delicate compound of rat poison, rot gut and broken bottles.

"Wrong number," I said.

"This is the right number, McGee. And you better have the right answers."

"Who is this?"

"Santa Claus. I got just one question and all I want is one answer—the right one. Where's Karen Lamain living?"

"Try the Missing Persons Bureau."

"That's the wrong answer. Take your choice. You can tell me the address of the building where you saw her with this K.L.B. or—"

"Or?"

"You fill in the rest."

"I'll fill it in all right, bub. I'll fill it in with this." I made the kind of mouth noise that doesn't always come from the mouth.

"That's two wrong answers, Jack. But I'm patient. You got till eight o'clock to get smart all of a sudden. After that—" He made the same noise back at me. "Get this number 'cause I'm giving it just once. Don't try tracing it, it's a public phone. Rhinelander 5-2506." He hung up.

I scrawled the number on the message pad. I didn't have the smallest idea what I'd do with it, but I took it down with the reflexes of any newspaperman.

There was one thing I did know. Whatever the boy with the broken-glass voice wanted from me he'd whistle long and hard for it. You don't stay in the news business very long after you begin revealing the sources of your information.

I walked back into the living room. The second call had awakened my local sleeping beauty. Maura had slipped on her stockings and a pair of blue silk garters.

She was climbing into the silver blouse when I entered.

"Don't you ever get cold wearing just that?" I asked.

"I've got my love to keep me warm," she sang. Dinah Shore didn't have anything to worry about, though.

Her eyes were bright and shining again and her voice had zing in it. I wasn't dying, but I didn't feel that frisky. "Hand me my skirt, Boyd darling." She went on humming the song. Four and a half hours was the most sleep she could have gotten. But this kid thrived on the things that killed anybody else.

She went into the john to straighten her hair and put on the blue skirt. I went into the bedroom and climbed into some clothes myself.

"Who was that on the phone the first time?" she called.

"You heard that?"

"Of course. It must have rung for ten minutes."

I took out a clean shirt and started removing the laundry pins. "So why didn't you answer it?"

"Don't be silly, darling. It just wouldn't look right to have me answering your phone." And of course this kid was really concerned about how things looked—in a pig's pores.

"The first call was from Calvin. The second was a mobster, I think."

"A what?" Her voice dripped fear. She walked in from the john still combing her hair. "A what?"

"Mobster. M-o-b-s-t—"

"You're joking." Her face was chalky. I stuck myself with a pin.

"Christ," I said. She hurried to me.

"Let me kiss it," she said. She smelled good.

"Let's not start that again," I said. I stuck my finger

in my mouth and sucked a drop of blood from it. When I took it out she kissed it anyway. I patted her on her blue velvet seat. There was something changed in her. A few hours earlier she was just an oversexed dame with too much money and an idea she could buy any bachelor bed in town. But the gray April morning changed that. Her eyes tried to hide a lonely, haunted look, but the mask wouldn't stay in place. Her full, lovely lips trembled at times, exposing a fear of the world that even her bankroll couldn't overcome. Funny, but I liked her more then, when I could see that she knew how to be frightened.

I walked back into the living room, slipping the shirt on as I went. She followed me, still combing and patting her hair. "Calvin said I knifed him in the back," I said.

She laughed. "Good. Calvin never had much backbone. This might help."

"The Smith guy he mentioned last night, you knew who it was all along?"

"Kingsley Benson. Calvin told me earlier. I was saving it for a surprise."

I nodded. "I wish you hadn't saved it, Maura. I carried an item in the column today about Benson and an ex-chorus girl. It's not going to help Benson fight his wife's divorce action."

"What of it, darling? You're a newspaperman. You write as you please, right?"

"Right. Only I don't print everything I know. Like I don't go around sticking guys for a million-dollar alimony, for example." I tucked in my shirt and headed back to the bedroom for a tie.

"Calvin doesn't bother me, though," I called. I found a blue polka dot job I liked and walked back to the living room. “That second call was a gravel-voiced crumb who wanted me to tip him to Karen Lamain’s address. He gave me ten hours to dig it up or make funeral arrangements.”

“Karen La—Lamain?” she stammered.

“Benson’s chorus girlfriend. Also the wife of a very bad citizen now in a New Jersey jail. Her married name is Whipper.” I finished the tie off and slipped into my suit jacket. “Charlie Whipper’s a professional blackmailer and God knows what. He’s only been jugged once and that time for knocking over a city bank in broad daylight.”

“But what makes you think that the one who called is a—”

“It figures. When Whipper got sent up he probably left some friends on the outside to see to it that his bride kept her legs crossed for good luck. This guy who phoned saw the item in this morning’s column and probably decided to squeeze her address from me and pay her a rough little call.” I pulled on my topcoat and nodded for her to do the same.

“What are you going to do now?” she whispered. We started out of the apartment and I tore the Rhinelander number off the memo pad as we went.

“I don’t know yet. M-G-M didn’t send me the rest of the script.”

Come to think of it, that whole morning smelled like a bad movie.

Outside the sky was overcast and I realized that the milkman and I had both been doing some wishful thinking about the weather. April was going to drop a few more wet forget-me-nots before she left town.

We walked a couple of blocks east looking for a cab,

and Maura said she was on her way uptown to finish arranging for a one-woman show of her paintings at a Fifty-seventh Street gallery. I whistled. Even a wiseguy columnist knows you've got to have something on the ball to get a solo showing. She explained that it helped when you had money. I told her that it always does, which it does.

We finally got her a cab and she gave me the address of her Beekman Place apartment. It was just after she left and I was walking back west to my breakfast joint that I became certain I was being tailed.

When we'd been walking east I thought that the green 1951 Pontiac that was crawling along behind us was just another car lost in Greenwich Village. But when I put Maura in a cab and started for the restaurant, the Pontiac turned and doubled back behind me.

I stopped at a haberdashery window and watched the reflection of the Pontiac stop with me. There were two young characters sitting in front, crisp white shirts and the same scrubby haircuts that Calvin Stockton wore. The only gun I owned was in my top bureau drawer protecting some socks and a carton of Chesterfields.

I straightened my tie in the shop window and waited for the college boys to make their move. I bent over and pretended to study the price tag on a pair of lavender shorts that the boys at Club 41 would have called "fabulous."

The scrub-heads talked things over in the car. The store next to the haberdashery was a record shop. A loudspeaker over the door blasted out a sad hillbilly tune called "Bury Me with My Hound Dawg at My Side." I straightened up and sidled over to the record shop. That's when the scrub-heads decided to make their play.

The driver nudged the car over to the curb and the other one hopped out and sauntered around the front, taking the sidewalk in one jump. If there's anything I like to meet before breakfast it's the junior varsity type who's still trying to win his letter.

The record shop window was dirtier than the haberdasher's, but I could make out the college boy's reflection approaching me. Three steps back he slowed and reached for his inside breast pocket. It was too bright and early for even this wet-eared punk to be making a gun play so I stood my ground. I turned and gave him a smile.

"Don't that hill music give you gooseflesh?" I asked.

I was one step from him now. If his hand didn't come out empty I figured to chop the gun with my right hand, swing my left foot behind his knee and follow through with a judo thrust that should have landed him on his prat.

That much was easy. What I wanted to know was whether the boy in the Pontiac would go on picking his teeth through all of it. I didn't have to worry. When the hand jerked from the jacket it came out with a wallet.

"McGee?" He flipped the wallet open. "State business. You got a couple of minutes?" The card in the wallet said "Official" and a few other things. I smiled and nodded.

"You boys didn't have to go to all this trouble. You could have gotten me at my office later. This cloak-and-dagger stuff just makes everybody jumpy."

He smiled back and returned the wallet. "Sorry, McGee. We had to move fast on this. Follow me."

I was at his heels when we started for the car, but he was behind me when we reached it. The kid knew his business better than I'd figured.

He motioned to me and I walked around to the other side of the car. I opened the door and held it for him, but he nodded again and I shrugged and slid into the front seat. Then he climbed in and the two scrub-heads sat like bookends squeezing me between them.

The driver took a pack of cigarettes from under the sunshade and offered them around. He was a gold-haired boy of twenty-two or so, with watery gray eyes and a deep cleft in his chin as if the sculptor's knife had slipped at the last minute.

"I'm Sloan," gray-eyes said, "and this is my partner, Kimberly Taylor."

"What's the pitch, boys?"

Taylor nodded to Sloan and the gray-eyed kid took the cigarette from his mouth and stared at the burning end for half a minute.

"McGee," Sloan began, "you've got a chance to be very helpful to an important government agency—state agency." He waited for me to say something.

"So?"

I wasn't being difficult; I just had nothing to go on.

Sloan took another drag on the butt and flipped it out the window. A pure waste of tobacco. Sloan wasn't comfortable. I figured he was better with his hands than his mouth.

"You see," he began again, "what's tough about this is that we can't let you in on the ground floor. You've got to trust us, right, Taylor?"

Taylor squirmed around to face me. Sloan wiped one palm on the arm of his soft gray flannel. He was glad to be out of it. "McGee, you're a man of varied experience," Taylor said. He was obviously the mouthpiece on the team.

Taylor talked in a monotone that matched the bored look in his eyes. His body was long and thin, but his hands were big red claws that he could probably use as well as his mouth. But mostly he was the mouthpiece.

"We won't beat around the bush. There's something going on down here in the city that has Governor Bellows upset. It's not a state catastrophe or anywhere near it, at the moment. But it could get out of hand. However, by its very nature, a mess like this has to be handled with soft gloves."

"A mess like what?" I asked. Taylor let one half of his mouth smile.

"That's what's so difficult. We need your help but we can't offer anything in return. Not even the knowledge of the value of your contribution. This is top secret!"

I arched my eyebrows. "Sounds like federal stuff."

"It could get that big unless we squash it at the source."

Taylor said. He nodded at Sloan again and gray-eyes picked it up from there. Taylor was the engineer. Sloan was the conductor.

"McGee," Sloan began, "you printed an item in this morning's column concerning Karen Lamain. You know who this woman is?"

"Ex-chorine, married to a thug named Whipper. She's probably been laying low since Whipper went to jail. She might be trying to escape a couple of maiden aunts Charlie left behind to keep an eye on her love life. Aunts that carry cannons."

"That's a good package," Sloan said. "That part about the aunts is new to Taylor and me. Might be worth a look, Kim."

Taylor flipped open a black notebook and scribbled something. "What you got is only half the study," Sloan went on. "This thing is dark and dirty. We need a lead on Karen Lamain. She's hiding out from us too. Your item about her was the first lead we've had in six months."

I figured it like this: little Karen got tired of waiting for Charlie to come home, so she decided to take in some dirty washing of her own. Whipper couldn't afford to keep her in nylons on the three-twenty a day New Jersey paid him for making license plates.

"I'll do whatever I can, boys," I said. "But you ought to know first that I've already had one call for Karen's address."

"The old-maid-aunts?" Sloan asked. I blinked my eyes. "Get a line on them?"

"A phone number. Public phone, probably." I searched through my pockets and then decided I'd left the number on the phone pad. I hadn't. It was right there in my right-hand jacket pocket. I don't know which one thing decided me. Maybe it was Taylor's big red hands, maybe Sloan's watery eyes or maybe just the way the two scrub-heads had of looking way above the job they were doing. The faint odor of old fish was there somewhere.

"I can dig it up for you later?" I said.

"How about now?" Sloan asked, with maybe a little hard stuff in his voice.

"Later will do," Taylor said. "But what about Karen's address? That's the big number, McGee. You pass it on now and we can move in there in twenty minutes."

"Sounds like short notice for a big operation," I commented.

"Our boys know every tick-tock of the way," Sloan said

"How about the address?" Taylor reminded me.

I gave it a light laugh. "Funny about that, I won't be able to turn it over to you for another hour. The truth is I don't have it." And that much was true. Sam hadn't told me just where on Madison Avenue he'd spotted the woman, and I hadn't had a chance to call him back on it. "Let me have your number and I'll call—"

Sloan gave the ignition key an ugly twist and bumped the car off in a hurry. "I told you this would be for the birds," he said.

He wheeled the Pontiac around the corner and into a narrow dead-end alley. Now I saw why the boys had decided to close in at the record shop. This back alley was real convenient. Three sides were covered by blank walls—no doors, no nothing. You could have started up a nudist colony there without attracting a crowd.

Taylor jumped out and stuck something in my ribs that felt harder than a finger and bigger than a pipe stem. I came out with both hands high. The whole play was crazier than hell.

"You guys been at this long?"

"Long enough," Sloan growled. He climbed out on the other side and came around to us. Taylor motioned me forward till I was between them and the car was between us and the mouth of the alley.

"We don't say you're in with them," Taylor said.

"And we don't say you're clean either," Sloan snarled.

"With whom? Clean of what?"

"That much you know," Taylor said. "In or out, you know that much."

Sloan took over again. "My guess is that you're in—

only for yourself, not them. You're smart, McGee. I know the type. Well, we're smart too." He gave me a fat open hand across the face. My nose started dripping red. That's the only part of me that bleeds easy. The rest you have to squeeze a little.

I yanked out a handkerchief and stuck it to my nose. "The minute you guys want to explain things, I'll listen. I'll even forget this nose business if it sounds good enough."

"Then see if you can forget this," Sloan said.

"Sloan!" Taylor shouted.

I turned to the sound of Taylor's voice and Sloan let me have it on the back of the skull. I pitched forward and caught the car radiator on the way down. I started to straighten up and Sloan stepped in and booted me a good one in the backside. I half-climbed up the radiator. Sloan grabbed me by the collar and pulled me down.

He was wide open for a knee, a rabbit punch or a plain old fist in the puss. But Taylor, too clean a boy for violence, stood to one side with his gun pointed at my chest while Sloan gave me a good going over—hard splatting blows to the back of the neck, a sting or two in the ears, a couple of whacks on the nose just in case the blood had begun to dry and a few other little things aimed at making my life uncomfortable without ending it permanently.

"Enough," Taylor yelled.

"Enough," I mumbled.

Sloan added a final ear clout and stepped back to admire his masterpiece. He was annoyed at all the blood I'd dropped on his gray flannel jacket.

The two climbed into their car and backed out of the alley. Taylor poked his head out of the window for a last happy message. "You won't get any cooperation out of the cops and you won't find our names in the regular State Police listing, McGee. So just forget about this. But keep thinking about what we need. Go easy on yourself, mister. We like to do business the other way, but we know this way as well as Whipper's boys. Hold out on us and we'll prove it." They drove off.

The whole thing was crazy. Cops don't treat newspapermen like that. Not unless they're either off their nuts or drunk on "Superman" juice. Those kids must have been both.

CHAPTER FOUR

Joe, the elevator boy, was off duty now and he was standing outside my apartment house looking up at the sky. He was out of uniform and looked kind of strange in his civvies. I looked even stranger.

"Brother!" Joe said. "What hit you, Mr. McGee?"

I batted my big brown eyes at him. "Why, whatever do you mean, Joseph? I thought this blue pinstripe I'm wearing was a pretty nifty number."

"It might have been. But right now it's got a rip down one side, a pocket torn out of the jacket and that collar looks like it's been through a mangler."

I inspected the jacket and made like I was shocked. "It's these cleaners they have nowadays. They don't seem to get anything right."

He laughed. "Yeah, I know what you mean. I ran into one of them *cleaners* once in a barroom on Third Avenue. He knocked out three of my teeth. See, up here on the side." He put a finger in his mouth and pointed to some bridgework. "Ith ri' back here," he said.

"Very handsome," I said. "Now that we understand each other, Joe, you can do me a favor. If any of those cleaning boys drop round to see me while you're on duty, tell 'em I stepped out for a pack of butts and I'll be back in five years." I picked up the torn piece of cloth that was hanging from my jacket pocket and tucked it inside.

"Got you. They won't get past me, Mr. McGee. Geeze, you sure have a good life. Hanging out with all those pretty dolls and celebrities and gangsters. Take me. Right now I'm trying to figure, should I go to the movies now and sleep this afternoon or should I sleep now and take in the pictures later. You sure have the life."

The torn pocket flopped out again and I thought, to hell with it. My stomach hurt where the car radiator had dug into it when one of the scrub-heads had booted me. I rubbed the pain, but it didn't help much. "Yeah," I said, "I sure got the good life."

I dragged myself upstairs and into a hot shower. That helped. A clean suit helped even more. It was eleven o'clock by then and I still hadn't swallowed my breakfast. But I wasn't hungry. So I mixed up some instant coffee and took it down hot and black. It tasted awful, but it put me back on my feet.

I knew what my next move was. That didn't take much thinking. I put the name Karen Lamain in my column five hours before and two characters had already threatened to shoot me on sight: Calvin Stockton's million-dollar client, and a gravel-voiced bum calling from a Rhinelander phone number. On top of that two scrub-heads from some state cop outfit were ready to bleed me dry for information about the same little daisy. Karen Lamain was my next move.

I dialed Sam Baniff's number and he climbed on the phone with a mouth full of cotton. Sam likes to sleep till noon when he's on the night tour.

"What'n hell time is it?" he gurgled.

"Noon," I said.

"Baloney. I don't feel like this at noon."

"So call me a liar for an hour."

"Okay, make it fast. I was having a big, beautiful dream about me and Marilyn Monroe when you called. Hurry up, I want to get back to Marilyn."

"Look, Sam, I can't explain it all now, but I've been a busy boy while you were snoring. Two guys promised me mayhem and two others delivered. All for the same reason. Sam, without naming names, what was the address of that Madison Avenue building where you picked up a certain brunette last night?"

"Cripes. Did they hurt you, Boyd?"

"They didn't help me much," I said.

"I'm sorry about, that."

"No use crying over spilled blood, feller. Just slip me the address and I'll be on my way."

"I mean I'm sorry I didn't warn you about her last night. I figured she'd be hot and I meant to tell you, only it slipped my mind."

"How come you figured it?" I asked. This man Baniff was a walking college. The more I knew him the more he amazed me.

"Simple," he said. "There's been a story kicking around about her old man Charlie for a while now. You know Whipper got sent up for a bank job."

"So?"

"So some of the boys started wondering, since when

does a blackmail artist start playing around with bank jobs? And such a crumby one, at that. I mean, only a kid or a dope-hound would try to knock over a big city bank single-handed in broad daylight. So there's been a little rumor running around about that."

This was beginning to sound interesting. Too interesting for a telephone talk. "Hold it," I said. "I want to hear all of this, nice and slow. But not now, Sam. Meet me in front of the office at twelve. We'll grab some breakfast together. Only give me that address first."

"Right. I don't know the number, but it's a big, gray apartment house on the southeast corner of Madison Avenue and Sixty-ninth. You can't miss it. There's a blue canopy in front of the door."

"Madison Avenue and Sixty-ninth, southeast corner, blue canopy. Check. Meet you at twelve in front of the office."

"Twelve?" He yawned.

"Right. And Sam …"

"Yeah?"

"Don't go back to Marilyn!" I yelled. He laughed and hung up.

I started out of the apartment three times before I made it all the way. The first time I came back to dig a memo blank out of the suit I'd been wearing when the scrub-heads climbed all over me. There was a Rhinelander phone number on the memo. The second time I made it to the door before I remembered that I was practically naked. I didn't have a gun.

I went back and dug my .45 automatic out of the desk drawer where I kept it. I got a permit for it about five years back when a guy who ran a wire service for a horse race syndicate didn't like some things I wrote about him. The police said I didn't need a gun, but they'd give me police protection.

So they sent two cops out with me one night while I toured the nightclubs and gathered stuff for my column. By three o'clock the cops were stewed to the ears. One of them pinched a hat check girl and poured a drink down her neckline. The other one socked the Chinese ambassador in the nose. So they gave me my gun permit and told me to stay away from cops.

I scooped up the gun and hustled out of the house and went over to my garage. There I climbed into my green convertible, pulled up my coat collar and let down the car top. It wasn't the coldest April day I can remember, but there wasn't another car top down in town. That's probably why I did it. I like to be different, even if it costs me pneumonia.

On the way up to Karen Lamain's place I thought over what Sam had started to tell me. I hadn't dwelt much on Karen's husband, Charlie Whipper, but it was about time that I did.

I met Charlie once. It was in a West Forty-second Street hotel, a grimy little joint with rooms the size of closets, yellow light bulbs and an airshaft instead of windows. This was way back before I'd gotten my first newspaper job. Charlie had an appointment to meet my friend at the hotel on business. My friend didn't have much stomach for that kind of deal so he asked me to handle it for him.

This friend was in show business. That's where we'd first met back in the thirties when I was a starving vaudevillian doing prat falls, tap dances and trapeze spins for a thin buck.... My friend wasn't starving. He spent fifteen years working his way up to the top and he finally made it. During that time he'd barnstormed the country playing Shakespeare, Shaw and a lot of junk nobody ever heard of then or since. And, like any guy on the move, he made some fast friendships. One of these bounced back at him from a place called Joplin, Missouri.

There was this sweet-young-thing of a waitress in Joplin who lent him her bed one night. They got very drunk. He did some foolish things. She dragged out an old Kodak Brownie and they took pictures of each other in the raw. That was the most foolish thing he did.

When my friend got to the top of the heap on Broadway his name was spread around a lot in the papers. It even got as far as Joplin. So I had to go over to this roach resort on West Forty-second Street with five thousand dollars in fives and tens to buy back the negative from Charlie Whipper. The sweet young thing in Joplin knew enough to get in touch with a top man in the extortion racket.

I don't like doing business with blackmailers. You'll say, "Who does?" But what I mean is, I don't like doing business with them even when they've got you over a barrel. The average chump who comes up against an extortion plot gets himself a bad case of the shakes and ends up by saying, "What the hell, it's just this once and only for a few bucks." Only it's never for once, or a few bucks. You buy back a picture from them and two months later you buy back another print of it and then another and another.

Finally you cough up a clot of blood and they give you back the negative and you go home broke but happy. You sleep good for the first night in a year. The next morning some happy character tells you how they can make copies of a negative and the one you burned may have a brother. You never get another good night's sleep.

I knew all that when I sat down to do business with The Whip. But it wasn't my picture, my career or my five thousand bucks. So I talked to him the way I'd been instructed to. He pulled out the photograph and asked for the five G's. I told him I wasn't buying just photos, I was in the negative business too. He said that would cost five times five.

I explained that my friend hadn't been on top long enough to get that fat. He said, "That's tough." I told him my friend stood a chance of grabbing a Hollywood contract and this might kill the chance. He said, "That's very tough." I told him my friend now had a wife and two curly-headed kids. Then I hit him over the head with a bridge lamp before he could say "tough" again.

I took the photograph and found the negative in his wallet. I never thought he'd be carrying it on him. He wasn't such a smart rat. Just a rat. That was my only run-in with Charlie Whipper. That was enough.

I thought about that while driving up to Karen's apartment and I wondered why a guy like Whipper would move out of his field into something like bank jobs. The underworld isn't much different from the one most of us live in. There are hard-working crooks and lazy ones. There are skilled crooks and plain day-laborer thieves. And when a crook gets himself a skill, a specialty, he stays with it. So you won't find a jewel thief turning counterfeiter any more than a diesel mechanic would show up at an operating room to perform brain surgery.

I couldn't make head or tail out of Whipper's bank job, so I decided to forget about it until I met Sam for breakfast. But there was somebody else who could straighten me out about Charlie Whipper's bank job if she wanted to cooperate. So the rest of the way up to her place I thought about Karen Lamain. I figured that if the gravel-voiced bum with the Rhinelander number had to squeeze her address from me it meant that she wasn't anxious to see him. Using gravel-voice as a blackjack I planned to beat a yard of information out of Whipper's wife.

I knew the apartment wouldn't be registered under her own name. So I told the doorman a romantic tale. It seems I saw this gorgeous wench in a restaurant one night and fell smack in love. I went there every night just for the sight of her and had even followed her home twice but I'd never had the courage to even speak to her. Now I'd decided I was a man, not a mouse. So if I just knew her name and apartment I'd go up there and plead my case. I punctuated the story with a few blushes, some silly grins and a dig or two in the ribs. The doorman must have been a romantic because he bought the whole line of goods. He even wanted to go up there and give me some moral support. I blushed three times more and stammered my way out of that.

I reached her apartment and stood before the door like it was the top of the Himalayas and I was this guy Tensing. When I recovered from the thrill, I rang the bell and waited. I rang again and waited some more. The third time around I realized she wasn't at home. That took some of the sweet taste out of it. But not all. I pulled out my key chain and got to work.

I've got about fifteen keys on the end of my chain. They're basic blanks that are used for most New York apartments. There's a guy on Thirty-fourth Street who can grind out those fifteen so they'll fit any lock in town. Only you've got to know the guy and show him the color of your money, five bucks a key. And don't let the Johns pick you up with them—they're a suspicious lot.

Karen Lamain's apartment turned out to be a quiet little affair, three rooms with a view of the avenue. The living room was a good-sized one and I figured the rent at a hundred and a quarter. That's no millionaire's rent, but you've got to do more than sit home knitting till your husband gets out of stir if you want to pay it off. So I nosed around the joint to see what kind of business Karen was in.

I had to pick the lock of her piano to find out. That piano was no piano. Where the soundboard and strings should have been Karen stored two small, compact sound amplifiers, the kind used for public address systems. Where the keyboard should have been she had microphones. Only they didn't look like microphones. One of them was camouflaged behind a paper rose. A man could wear it in his lapel, a woman in her hair. Another one was the size of a penny and the thickness of a bottle cap. It was built into a wristwatch case. There were a couple of others that could be planted in flower pots, chandeliers, toilet bowls, etc.

Karen Lamain was in her husband's trade. She was a blackmailer. A twentieth-century, wired-for-sound blackmailer.

It might have been that Charlie left a couple of boys on the outside when he went into the can to keep an eye on Karen's love life. But this business of the mikes and amplifiers suggested a better possibility. If Karen was plying her old man's trade, chances were she was using his sucker list. Charlie might not mind, but his boys wouldn't take to it kindly. Especially if they weren't getting a cut of the melon. I liked that money angle better than the love one. With people like Karen and Charlie love is reserved for money.

I closed the piano up and gave the rest of the place a quick eye. Karen owned some ten-dollar Scotch, some Paris gowns, a lot of sheer underwear and a dozen pair of nylons. She also owned a packet of letters with a New Jersey street return address that I recognized as the state penitentiary. The letters were tucked under the nylons. They let the prisoners use that street address so that their neighbors, who watched them being led down the street in manacles with two of the local *polizei*, won't suspect a thing.

I went through the letters quickly. They read more like a soldier's letters home than notes from a cell: complaints about the chow, stories about the boys he was bunking with, requests for cigars, candy, magazines and so forth. Pretty dull stuff. There was one thing that ran through all the letters and nudged my interest, something that seemed out of place. Every letter had a line or two about "our baby."

One read, "Take care of our little baby." Another one ran, "How's baby getting along?" Another, "I miss the baby. Can't wait to see the little feller." It was like that in every letter.

I stuffed the letters back under the nylons and closed the bureau drawer on the touching contents. It was eleven forty by then and I had a date with Sam at twelve. I gave the apartment one more tour before leaving. Something kept gnawing at me. In the three rooms, through the kitchen. living room and bedroom, in closets and bureaus, on chairs and laundry rack, there wasn't one stitch of baby clothes. Charlie Jr. must have been a naked little rascal.

I locked up the place and drove back downtown. I hadn't learned very much about Charlie Whipper's reasons for turning from blackmail to bank jobs, but the trip hadn't been a total loss. For one thing, I got a good line on how Karen was keeping the wolf from her door. She was beating him off with camouflaged microphones. For another, I learned about the Whipper's little boy, a kid that lived without clothes, bottles, cribs, carriages or Dy Dee dolls. It was all highly educational. But what the hell did it mean?

I made good time driving back and I got down to Forty-seventh Street by five of twelve. I put the car in a parking lot and walked over to the office. I had a minute or two to spare so I put them to use along the way. There was a memo blank with a Rhinelander phone number burning a hole in my pocket. So I dropped into a drugstore and called a number down on Centre Street, Police Headquarters. There's a police lieutenant down there named Fred who used to be a captain of police. Fred made one mistake in his cop career: he locked up a guy who ran down three school kids with his car one Friday morning. The guy in the car was drunk and one of the kids damn near died. But locking that bum up was Freddie's last act as a police captain. The bum was a city councilman's son-in-law.

So Fred is a lieutenant now and spends most of his time reading detective stories and sweating out the two years between him and his pension. I gave Fred a good break in my column when that business with the drunken driver came up and we've been kind of chummy ever since.

What I wanted from him this time was a tracer on that Rhinelander phone number. In New York if you've got a guy's name and address and you need his phone number all you do is dial Information. But if you've got his phone number and what you want is his name and address, you'd better know a guy like Fred at headquarters because you couldn't beat it out of Information.

Fred took down the number and told me to ring back in fifteen minutes. I swung out of the drugstore and across town to the office. It was five after twelve when I got to the building and Sam still wasn't there. I figured he might have had trouble finding a parking space at that hour, so I lit a cigarette and waited around.

It couldn't have been more than three minutes later that I spotted Sam's hack tearing down the street. I figured that he was cruising around looking for a parking space. I waved to him. He didn't wave back. He passed me doing fifty or sixty and tore through a red light. I stood there with my jaw hanging down while I watched Sam Baniff, one of the shrewdest hackies in town, breaking half a dozen traffic laws in the middle of Manhattan at high noon.

And then I saw the other car. It was a dark green Cadillac with white walls and lots of chrome. It was doing fifty or sixty too. It broke through the traffic light after Sam, overtook him halfway down the next block and started nudging him to the side.

I took off on the run. I made it across the street, dodging traffic all the way, when I heard the noise. It came three times in quick succession. It sounded like somebody was cracking one of those toy whips you buy at the rodeo. But it was no whip. It was a gun.

Sam's cab did a half turn, climbed up the curb and rammed into a building. The front wheels started up the side of the building like they were prepared to climb it if Sam gave the word. The cab rested there for a split second and then rolled over and crashed to the sidewalk. When I got there it was lying on its side and the wheels were still spinning. Sam and his cab were cut from the same steel. They both quit hard.

I ran out into the street and tried to make out the license tag on the Caddy as it roared off. Fat chance.

When I got back to the cab a crowd had collected and half a dozen guys were standing around talking about whether they should try to turn the cab back over or should they wait for the ambulance or the cops or the coroner. And all the while they were jawing away, Sam's life was probably leaking out of him. I pitched off my overcoat, screamed a few curses at the talkers and started climbing up the belly of the cab.

I made it all right and managed to get the front door open. I stood there looking down into the cab at Sam's bloodied face. He wasn't dead. He gave me a smile and lifted one finger from the wheel. That's where his hands were, still on the wheel.

I wanted to climb down inside there but I was afraid I'd fall all over him. I didn't know just how bad he'd gotten it but from where I stood it didn't look good. I got down on my haunches and pushed my head through the doorway.

"Don't try to talk," I said. "Blink your eyes once for yes, twice for no." He blinked once. "Is it bad?" He blinked once. "Where, in the gut? The steering wheel catch you in the gut?" He blinked twice for no. "The ribs?" He blinked twice again. There was blood all over him, from his chest down to his shoes. "The chest?" He didn't bother blinking this time. He just rolled his head over sideways. Up to then all I could see was the right side. He rolled it over to the left and I saw where he'd gotten it. The whole left side of his face was torn open. It must have been a cannon that hit him. They don't make bullets that big.

I knew he was done for. Blood bubbled out of his nose and he was choking on it. I pulled my head out of the doorway and screamed down at the crowd, "Where the hell's the ambulance?" Somebody yelled something back, I don't know what. I didn't much care. The ambulance talk was strictly for Sam's benefit. Then I leaned in over the doorway again, grabbed one edge of the frame with both hands and let myself down into the cab slowly. If Sam was going to die, it wouldn't be alone.

He was lying against the left front window through which you could see the pavement maybe an inch or two below. I couldn't just sit beside him or I'd have mashed what was left of him to an ugly pulp. So I had to support myself by holding on to the back seat with both hands and thrusting up the way you do a side-stand on an exercise bar.

"Look, Sam," I said, "you're going to be okay, see? You got marked up a little, but you're going to be okay." He smiled to show me that he knew better. I went on with the lie. "But even though you're going to be fine, it's important that you tell me who did this. Tell me now, Sam. The docs might have you full of sleep pills for days. Who did it, Sam?"

He opened his mouth. Blood belched out. I released one hand and yanked out my breast pocket handkerchief. I wiped some of the blood from his mouth. He blinked once and then tried to talk once more. The blood gurgled in his throat. It was like trying to talk under water. At first nothing came out, just a lot of hissing and gurgling sounds. Then he made a *k* sound and kept repeating it. “K—k—k—k—” Then he said, “Karen”—almost that clear too—and his head rolled over and he was gone.

The blood stopped pumping out of him in a minute. I wiped the mess around his mouth and chin once more and then dropped the handkerchief on the floorboard. I turned to climb back out when this big, bluff voice bellowed down at me.

“You down there. Come on up. What n’hell are you doing down there to begin with?” It was a cop talking—a big, beefy-faced cop.

“I’ve been at a funeral,” I said, kind of low.

“What?” he shouted.

“Nothing,” I said, and started hoisting myself out of there.

“All right, all right,” the cop said when I’d pulled myself above the door. “Now what business did you have down there?” That seemed like a joke so I laughed.

“Look, officer,” I said, “there’s a guy dead in there. A minute ago he could have used an ambulance but there was no ambulance. Now we need a crane but there’s no crane. And all you can think of is to stand around asking questions? Aw, come on, buddy, you can do better than that.”

The thick, black fur of his eyebrows creased into an angry V. “First,” he hissed, “I ain’t your buddy. Second, there’s an ambulance on its way. Third, I already sent for a hoist. And fourth, what the hell were you doing in there?”

I gave him a quick rundown without telling him

more than I thought he ought to know. I told him I was standing on this corner waiting for this friend of mine when this cab came along and then this Caddy, and then there were some shots and by the time I'd climbed inside, the hackie was dead. That's all I told him. I didn't mention the fact that this particular cabby was a pal of mine. I didn't say anything about having an appointment with him to receive some information about a blackmailer serving time for a bank job. And most of all, I didn't say anything about the one word that Sam had spoken before he died.

The flabby-faced cop with the bushy eyebrows seemed satisfied and I climbed back down from the cab. The crowd was pretty thick by then and I recognized a couple of the boys from my paper. One of them was a police reporter, the other was a photographer, named Jones. I decided to give them both the slip. The cop standing on the cab spotted me before I could take off.

"You there," he called. "Hang around. There'll be some more questions. Just stay where you are."

So Jones and the police reporter spotted me and walked over. I gave them the same story I'd handed to the cop. I figured that Jones would see through it later. He knew Sam Baniff and he knew that the guy had worked for me. But right then I didn't care about that. So long as I could just get out of there and forget for a couple of minutes, forget Sam lying there with blood bubbling out of him, forget the gurgling sound his voice made when he tried to talk, forget how he looked with one side of his face squashed in.

Jones wanted to get up on the car and take a shot of the body. The cop didn't like the idea. The police brass hadn't arrived yet, the lab men, the coroner and the rest. The cop was afraid to breathe until they got there. So Jones had to content himself with a few shots of the car. I didn't try to slip off again. Before Jones spotted me it would have been safe enough. But once the cop had a lead to me it was useless.

So I waited around until the ambulance arrived and then the cop brass and more newspapermen and maybe a thousand interested parties. Jones was still running around trying to get permission to shoot the body. The cop with the furry eyebrows brought me over to the captain in charge and he put a few questions to me. I gave him the same answers I'd given the first cop. I continued withholding the fact that I'd known the dead man or anything about him. The captain seemed satisfied with that. They took my name and address and released me.

As I started out of the crowd, I could see Jones climbing up on the cab with his camera and bulbs. I quickened my pace. I almost made it, too. It was just as I'd reached the last ring of cops on the fringe of the crowd that Jones stood up on the cab, looked in the open door and then turned to wave to me. "Hey, Boyd. It's Sam! It's your friend, Sam Baniff!"

A cop grabbed me from the front and another from behind. They lifted me off the ground and carried me back through the crowd.

"Withholding evidence," one said.

"Running from the scene of an accident," the other said.

"Resisting arrest," the first said.

"Tampering with the material evidence of a crime," the other said.

"Let me down easy, boys," I said. "I've had a rough morning." And all the while I kept seeing Sam's face floating in front of me, the blood bubbling from it, the life ebbing away.

CHAPTER FIVE

The police captain who already questioned me had the two cops walk me over to his car. They stuck me in the back seat, the captain on one side and a plainclothesman on the other. The flabby-faced cop who'd been the first on the scene sat in the front seat facing back at me.

The captain nodded at flabby-face and the cop went into his act.

"I'm on traffic duty, Forty-seventh and Broadway. These two cars, the cab and this big, green job, came tearing across from Sixth Avenue a couple of minutes ago. They broke through the light and tore on west. I tried to whistle them down but they buzzed right along. So I started running after them. By the time I got to Eighth Avenue I heard these shots and a crash. I got to a call box and turned in the alarm.

"When I got to the cab it was lying on the sidewalk like it is now. I climbed up to get a look inside and I see this guy down there with the driver of the car. I never saw him climb in. I don't know, maybe he went in after the smash-up like he says, maybe he was in there all along. He gave me the same story he handed you, Captain. He never said nothing about knowing this hackie. He withheld evidence, that's one thing sure."

A thin, pale-faced little man carrying a black satchel poked his head into the police car. "Looks like the bullet killed him, not the crash. I'll be able to tell better when we get him downtown. Figures to be a .45 slug. Entered at the left ear, straight across the face and out through the left nostril. He might have lived a minute or two, I can't tell. That slug made a mess of his face. His own mother wouldn't recognize him from the left side."

The captain nodded and the thin man with the satchel left.

"So tell us about it," the plainclothesman said. He might have been anywhere between twenty-five and forty. He had one of those lean, freckled faces with a shock of red hair. He had a face that never seems to grow old.

I told them about it. This time I admitted knowing Sam and admitted having an appointment with him. All I withheld now was the reason for the appointment and that single word Sam had spoken.

"You can do better than that," the freckle-faced detective said. "All you're telling us is what we already know and you're only telling that because you know we know it. Now tell us something new."

I said there was nothing new. The captain asked me to go over it again. I read it through a second time, sticking close enough to the first version to cover myself and not so close as to make it sound memorized. They weren't satisfied.

"Look," Freckles said. "Before we knew who you were and who that dead man was we accepted your story. Now we know both and we don't buy it. You see, we know Baniff worked for you. We know you printed an item in your column this morning about a certain ex-chorine who's married to a con. We know that there are some of this con's pals around town who're anxious to find this girl. And we got reason to believe that it was Baniff who tipped you to her. Now what do you say about that?"

I got real talkative. I said, "Huh?"

Freckles ran it down all over again. And while he was repeating himself I had time to think. I figured that the two scrub-heads from the state police, or wherever, must have been working pretty close with the local Johns on this thing. From what those two knew and from what the cops already had on Sam and me, they were able to get pretty close to it now. So I figured the best thing to do was to level with the law and try to come to terms.

"Okay," I said. "You're right on top of it. Sam was the one who tipped me to Karen Lamain. I did get a call from some crumb who promised me a coffin if I didn't kick in with Karen Lamain's address. Only I didn't know it then and I wouldn't have kicked in if I did."

"But you do now?" That was the captain. He was a middle-aged man with twinkly brown eyes and a fedora that matched them. He had a nervous habit of running his fingertips up along his neck and under his chin like he was always checking to see how good the last barber had shaved him. "You know her address, now?"

I nodded. "That's right. And if you'll give me twenty-four hours I'll know a hell of a lot more than that. I'll know what makes a guy like Charlie Whipper turn from blackmail to bank jobs. I'll know where Karen Lamain is planting her little microphone these days. And, most of all, I'll know the rat who gunned Sam." Giving myself that deadline was spreading it a little thick, but I had to take that chance.

The funny thing is, they didn't say a word about the deal. They didn't say a word about anything else except Karen Lamain. That part really interested them. Almost as much as Karen interested the two scrub-heads. So now I knew what my trump card was.

"What was that about this Lamain dame and some microphones?" the plainclothesman asked. He pushed his freckled face close to mine and got extra chummy. "What about her, Boyd?"

"I'll bite," I said. "What about her, Herman?"

"The name is Pete," he said. "And I'm doing the asking." His face got flushed and some of the freckles disappeared into the general redness of the skin. "Now give. Where is this Lamain woman and what was that crack about microphones?"

"Two very good questions," I said. I lit a cigarette and stared out the window of the car. Freckles got impatient. The captain motioned for him to simmer down. And then we waited. I waited, the captain waited, Freckles waited, the flabby-faced cop waited. Everybody waited. Freckles was the first to crack.

"God damn it," he said, "why are we treating him with kid gloves? He's broken the law. We've got enough now to make it rough. Why are we playing it so fancy?" There were a couple of answers to that. One of them was obvious. Being a newspaperman, I got special treatment from the Department. They'll deny it from now till next July, but cops are as publicity conscious as a Hollywood starlet. There was another reason too.

The captain didn't say anything. The flabby-faced cop didn't say anything. So I did. "You're new at this, Pete. If you weren't you'd know why the captain here is playing it soft. You want something from me, right, Pete? You want me to be real friendly and supply you with some information, right, Pete? So how're you going to make me real friendly, with a rubber hose, maybe? Or a piece of pipe?" I shook my head.

Pete looked from the captain to me and then back to the captain. His face paled now and the freckles boiled up to the surface. "Is that it, Captain? Has this guy got us by the short hairs?"

The captain made a fist with one hand and opened the palm of the other as though he was going to drive the two together. Then he closed his eyes and his lips moved. After a minute he relaxed the fist and shoved both hands into his pants pockets. He stared out the window not saying anything for a while. When he talked his voice was way off in space somewhere, out the window and over the city.

"Used to be a man could run his own department. Used to be you'd work your fanny off for twenty years so you could end up giving the orders and damn well know they'd be carried out. Now they've got State men and Federal men and Treasury men and God knows what. And all of them not more than kids. Punks." He spat out the window. Then he opened the door and got out.

He looked fat, standing there in the doorway. Middle-aged and fat. But the kind of fat you wouldn't want to tangle with, even when it's middle-aged. "Give him his twenty-four hours," he said. "Give him any damn thing he wants. I'm going home and get drunk."

He walked off with a bow-legged step like he was wearing wet drawers—as if walking was as painful as cancer.

I understood now. I wasn't the only one the scrub-heads had roughed up. They used a gun and knuckles on me. They'd used something nearly as hard on the captain—authority. They beat me up on the outside. They beat him up on the inside. Maybe he deserved it, I didn't know. But right then I figured that any enemy of the scrub-heads was a friend of mine.

After that Freckles and I came to terms. The department was under orders to get a lead on Karen Lamain. I had that lead. I agreed to turn over her address the following day. In return they agreed to release me and let me operate unhampered. I didn't expect any cooperation from them. Just some freedom to operate. I gave Freckles something in return to bind the deal, the Rhinelander phone number. But I didn't tell him that it was a public phone. And I didn't say he'd have to call at eight o'clock on the head and ask for a man with a voice like broken bottles. I wasn't going to earn his full pay for that week.

When I got out of the car they were carrying Sam away. The hoist had righted the cab and lifted it out into the street. The radiator was stoved in and both front lights were smashed, but it didn't look half as bad as you'd imagine. You'd never have guessed that a great guy had just died in there.

I picked up my coat and started pushing my way out of the crowd. I was halfway out when one of the men who'd been standing around talking while Sam was dying in the cab fingered me. He was a big guy and a yard wide.

"That's him," I heard him say. "The cops had him for questioning. They think he was the one who bumped the cabby."

I was walking toward him. I kept going right on past him. Two steps past. Then I turned around and let him have it, just once, in the jaw. He stumbled back about six feet and fell to the pavement. Jones, the photographer, rushed in and grabbed my arms. "Come on, Boyd. Come on, feller," he said. I threw his hands off me.

"Lemme go," I yelled. "That's my boy they killed. That's my boy, Sam."

"Sure, sure," Jones said. He started leading me out of the crowd. I broke from him again and went over to where the big guy was lying on the ground. I leaned down. He doubled his fists and leered up at me.

"You'd never have done it if my back wasn't turned," he said.

"You're right," I said. "And look, I'm sorry about it. I kind of lost my head." He waited a minute to make sure he'd gotten it straight. Then he put out his hand and we shook.

I took one last look at the spot on the pavement where they still hadn't scrubbed off the blood and then walked off.

I walked back to the office, thinking about Sam, trying to get it straight that he was gone now. I knew that would take a while.

The cops had a theory about the killing. Freckles had outlined it in the car. He figured that the crumb who threatened to kill me if I didn't turn over Karen Lamain's address might have killed Sam for the same reason. I couldn't see that. How much information can you get out of a dead man?

But suppose they hadn't killed Sam for refusing to talk. Suppose they killed him because he was going to talk, but to the wrong people. Me, for instance.

Sam was on his way to give me an earful about Charlie Whipper. If the crumb who called from the Rhinelander number was one of Charlie's boys he wouldn't want Sam to deliver his message. He could have figured out, the way the cops did, that it was Sam who tipped me to Karen Lamain's address. And he could have figured that a guy with Sam's eyes and ears would know a little something about Whipper's bank job.

That's what Whipper's boys were trying to hush up. That's what Sam died for. By the time I reached my office I knew how to get Sam's killer. Get the guy with the Rhinelander number. That was the order of the day.

I phoned Fred down at police headquarters. I didn't ask him right off what luck he'd had tracing the Rhinelander number. I wanted him to know how things stood between me and the cops. I knew Fred wasn't exactly well liked down at headquarters. I didn't want him sticking his neck out for me. Not with only two years between him and his pension.

"This captain," Fred said, "was he a heavy-set guy around fifty with a worried look and a walk like he's got the clap?"

"That's the captain," I said.

"Fallon," he said. "Tim Fallon. He got that walk from riding too many horses back in the old mounted days. He's okay, though. If he gave you his word he'll stay with it."

"I didn't get the word from him. It was from a young, freckle-faced detective named Pete."

"That would be the redhead who follows up on Fallon. I know him too. Trust him like you would a coiled snake, Boyd."

"Right," I said.

"Now here's the line on that Rhinelander number—"

"Wait, Fred, you didn't get me. I said I'm playing this without the cops. The commissioner might not like it if you—"

He sighed. "Got a pencil?" I told him I did. "The

phone is registered to a Walter Blake, 519 East 68th Street. It's a barber shop over by the river. Blake was picked up once for running a horse parlor. Suspended sentence. That's all."

I thanked him. He was putting his neck on the block for me and a dead hacky named Sam whom he'd never even known. That's a pretty good friend. I thanked him twice. He brushed right past it.

"If you've got any good mysteries over at the office, send 'em on down," he said. "You know the kind I like."

I said, "Yeah," and hung up. I knew the kind he liked, stuff that was written back in the twenties and thirties, Chandler and Hammett and that crowd. He didn't think any detective stories worth their price had been written after 1942. That was the year Fred recommended an indictment for drunken driving against a city councilman's son-in-law.

I hung around the office the rest of the afternoon, reading mail, checking a couple of anonymous tips for the column. Nothing much. Columnists get unsigned letters like movie stars get fan mail. They're about as helpful too. I don't trust anything I don't pay for.

Most of my tips cost me the price of a good bottle of rye. A good one is worth half a case. More than half that money goes to hotel managers, airport and railroad clerks, taxi drivers, head waiters and so forth. People in a position to know who's leaving or coming to town, who buys dinner for whom, who's signing hotel registers "Mr. and Mrs. Smith."

I am not the only columnist who works that way. Most of them do. The only difference between me and most of the really big ones is that I don't have any salaried investigators, not even a secretary except the one the paper supplies to handle mail. I like to play it solo. You get lonely, but you're never disappointed.

I grabbed a sandwich in the office and worked through till seven-thirty. I didn't get a hell of a lot done. Something kept coming between my eyes and whatever I happened to be reading or writing at the time. It was Sam's face. Sometimes he'd be smiling. Sometimes he'd be laughing, big, broad, with that one gold tooth on the side of his mouth twinkling up at me. But mostly I saw his head resting against the cab window, the blood bubbling front his nose.

At seven thirty I picked up my hat and coat, crammed some notes into my pocket and took off. I drove the car out of the parking lot and headed uptown and east. I had a date in a barber shop with a guy who had broken bottles in his voice. This particular barber had a phone with a Rhinelander number. I was hoping that the guy I had the date with owned a gun, the gun that killed Sam. I wanted a chance to use it on him.

CHAPTER SIX

The barber shop was a block from the river. It was a slum block, two lines of brown and gray fire traps separated by a narrow, dirty gutter. The garbage was piled up in cans, boxes and bags from one end of the block to the other. I spotted three empty whiskey bottles within fifty feet of each other. It was a great place to bring up kids.

There were half a dozen guys sitting around in the barber shop when I walked in. They might all have been waiting for a shave but they weren't. They were playing seven-card stud. That's a lousy game.

One of the six guys was wearing a cotton jacket that must have been white once. I figured him for the barber. He was dealing. I coughed.

"You want a shave?" He didn't even look up from the cards.

I said, "Yeah."

He dealt around the board, calling the cards as they fell. "Two ladies here … Pair of threes … Still nothing … Possible straight …" I coughed. He dealt himself a deuce. He had a pair of fours on the board. He laughed. "Three of a kind." It was seven-card stud with deuces wild. That's the lousiest game there is.

He started dealing the last card down. I coughed again. I could have had galloping TB, it wouldn't have raised an eyebrow. I wanted to hear somebody talk, somebody with a voice that sounded like it had broken bottles in it. But nobody said a word. They picked up their last cards, one by one, turning up just the corners of them to spot the suit and number.

The guy with the queens bet fifty cents. The guy with threes threw his hole card up and cursed. The guy with nothing on the board raised the queens a half dollar. The others took another fast look at his open cards. Nothing. A king, a five, an eight, a ten and a three, with only two in the same suit. It looked like the worst bluff since that little boy who cried, "Wolf!"

The guy with the possible straight, ten high, called the raise. The barber looked at his pair of fours plus the wild deuce and then he bet right into the bluff. He raised it a buck. The bluffer called. The possible straight dug down for extra cash, and called. They turned over their cards.

The possible straight had made his. The barber had a pair of nines in the hole—full house. The bluffer wasn't bluffing. He had a five and eight of hearts on the board, a seven and nine in the hole, both hearts, and a deuce. Straight flush. That's what I like about seven-card stud.

They were all yelling at once, pounding the table, slapping the cards and kicking up a general stink. The table bounced, cards and glasses jumped with the vibration. A shot glass bounced off the table and fell to the floor.

"No go! We said no wild cards on straights and flushes. You know God damn well we said that, you crook!"

"No wild flushes. We played that way now for a year. What the hell's the matter with you?"

"Four-flushin' bastard. Touch the money and I'll cut your ears off." That was the barber. Some barber.

I was looking for a guy who had broken bottles in his voice. First these lice wouldn't talk and I was up a tree. Now the whole pack of them were talking and it was even worse. Every one of those crumbs had broken bottles in his voice.

I started out of the place and the noise stopped suddenly. I looked back. The six of them were staring daggers at me. One nodded to the barber. The barber said, "We ain't never seen you here before. Where you goin', Mac?"

"Up the avenue for a bite to eat," I said. "I'll be back."

The guy who nodded and the barber shrugged now. The barber turned back to me. "Okay. Make it twenty minutes. Give you the best shave in town."

"I'll bet," I said, and walked out. I could still hear them arguing halfway up the block.

Around the corner I found a cigar store. It was five past eight. I went inside and dialed the Rhinelander number. Somebody picked up the phone in the barber shop and I could still hear the yelling.

"This is McGee," I said.

"You're late," he said. That's all he said. I needed to hear more. All those broken bottles sounded so much alike.

"The hell," I said. "I called you five minutes ago and there was no answer. You must have been beating your wife or something. You didn't hear the phone."

"Yeah," he said. "Yeah, that could be. It was noisy here." Those were the right bottles. I had my man. "You got that address, McGee?"

"Sure," I said. "I'm no *shmo*. You think I'd let somebody kick my head in to protect some dizzy dame I never even met?"

"Smart," he said. "Okay, let me have it."

"Sure. Only you'll have to hold on a minute. I got it in the other room."

"On the double," he said. I put down the phone and walked out of the booth.

"Hey," the proprietor yelled. "You didn't hang up the phone."

"Leave it," I said. "I'm still talkin'. I'm just goin' out to spit." He nodded. He was an old cigar smoker. He knew how it was with spit.

I hotfooted it around the corner and back to the barber shop.

I walked inside.

"You're back early," the barber said.

"I couldn't wait for the best shave in town," I said.

There was a man on the telephone. But he wasn't talking to anybody. He was waiting. It was the guy who tried to bluff the deuces-wild flush.

"Sit down," the barber said. "I'll only be a few

minutes. Hey, Hauptman, get off the phone, you stinkin' bluff-artist."

Hauptman waited another minute and then hung up. He came back to the table. "Louse," he said. "Hung up on me. Louse." The cigar man must have figured I wasn't coming back from my spit.

"She pretty?" one of the others asked. Hauptman smiled.

"Real pretty," he said. Someone started dealing again. Hauptman picked up his money. "Count me out," he said. "Any place they cheat a guy out of a perfectly good straight flush ain't—"

"Cheat!" the barber yelled. "Look who's talkin'. How many times you yourself said, 'No straights or flushes on wild cards?' How many, huh?"

"Drop dead," Hauptman said and walked out. The barber laughed. I turned to go. "Hey," the barber called. "What about the shave?"

"Changed my mind," I said. "I'm gonna grow a beard."

I stood in the doorway and lit a cigarette while I watched Hauptman walk west. He turned left at the corner. I started west on the double. At the corner I slowed and bent as if to tie a shoelace. Hauptman didn't look back so I took off again. I gave him a full block lead. The streets were almost empty. That made it easy for me to keep an eye on him and vice versa. But Hauptman was too busy pushing his brain cells around to be on the lookout for a tail.

I knew what he was thinking about. He was on his way back to give a report, maybe to a partner, maybe to a boss. Either way the report wasn't going to be well received. Hauptman's chicken had flown its coop. I was the chicken.

We walked south to Fifty-eighth Street and then over to Lexington. I knew the territory well. There were half a dozen of those supper clubs that cafe society likes to sup-and-sip in located around there. That was practically the heart of my beat. It didn't seem like Hauptman's home grounds, though.

I had a surprise coming to me. That was not only Hauptman's neighborhood, but the door he turned in at was one of the richest spots in town, a place called La Fez. Nice little hole, La Fez, original Picasso paintings on the wall, original Paul Revere silverware on the sideboard and very original prices on the menu. In fact, no menu. Just waiters who advised you what to eat. Waiters who must have been former jewelers. One look at your cuff links and tie pin and they knew whether to recommend the thirty, forty or fifty-dollar dinner. That was four-flusher Hauptman's hangout.

I watched him walk in. He called the doorman by his first name. The doorman called him back by his first name. That's how I knew Hauptman worked there. It took one second's thought to realize just where he worked in La Fez.

Hauptman was no man of the world. He couldn't serve up a crepe suzette, he couldn't light a baked Alaska, he couldn't speak French. French, hell, he couldn't speak English. So Hauptman was no waiter in a place like La Fez.

La Fez was more than a high-class eatery, it was a cover for a gambling house, roulette wheel, chuck-a-luck, craps, *chemin de fer*, the works. But the croupiers who worked out on the second floor of La Fez were even classier than the waiters on the first floor.

The man who handled the wheel called the numbers in three languages. The gentleman at the craps table was third in line to the royal seat of a country in East Europe—if the royal family ever got its seat back. The man who pitched the cards for *chemin de fer* was an expert on statistics and had written a book called *Investments, Security or Risk?* That wasn't Hauptman's speed, either.

There was just one spot for Hauptman in the organization of La Fez. The first floor was a restaurant for rich internationals. The second floor was a gambling joint for the same expensive trade. The third floor was the boss' office. That was Hauptman's speed.

Pete Kincaid was the boss of the works at La Fez. He looked like a school teacher. He talked like a businessman. He dressed like the Duke of Windsor. He was a crook.

What Al Capone was to the twenties, Pete Kincaid was to the forties and fifties. Where Capone ruled a gang of coarse, broken-nosed, diseased gunmen who highjacked, bootlegged and murdered for a living, Kincaid invested his money wisely in garages, junkyards, real estate, prize fighters, record companies, race horses and many enterprises nobody will ever know about. But there was one thing in common to the working methods of Capone and Pete Kincaid—violence.

On the surface, Kincaid's investments were those of almost any law-abiding businessman, with the possible exception of the race horses and prize fighters. And even those have become pretty respectable, what with the Vanderbilts racing horses and the Hollywood crowd buying up fighters. But below the surface Kincaid had to use the same steel that built Capone's empire. If Kincaid had been born into money he could have worn the velvet with the best. But when you steal your first hundred thousand, you have to be ready to kill to hold on to it.

I had sampled Kincaid's food and played his wheel and whistled at the silver and crystal on the first two floors. But I'd never had reason to visit Pete's personal office, or the muscle men who reported in there. I'd managed to postpone that delight up until then. But all good things run out in time. And this was the time.

The doorman gave me a nod and called me "Mr. McGee." The headwaiter did the same except he said "*Monsieur*." The kid who ran the elevator offered me a tip on a hot Hollywood divorce story. I told him to save it till I was ready to leave. He said he couldn't take me straight up to Kincaid's office. I'd have to see Harry, the croupier, first. Harry's the one who wrote the book on investments.

I got off on the second floor. The wheels were spinning, the cards clicking, the dice rolling and the money was pouring in. There were about a hundred people getting happily clipped. It was still early in the evening.

Harry, a thin, wispy-haired man around forty with steel-rimmed glasses, sharp features and the delicate hands of a surgeon, gave me a silent greeting with his eyes as I neared the *chemin de fer* table. He turned the bank over to an assistant and came around the table.

"Pleasant surprise, McGee," he said without a smile. Come to think of it, I'd never seen Harry smile. "Business or pleasure?"

"Mostly business," I said. He nodded.

"The drinks are on the house, but you'll have to buy your own chips."

"It's not that kind of business," I said. "I want to see

Kincaid."

He nodded again and didn't bother asking what for. He was a man of few questions. Instead he flipped open a little brown book he carried in his jacket pocket and traced his fingers over a page. "There's an opening from ten to ten thirty. After that you'll have to wait till closing time. That's two." He snapped the book shut and tucked it back in his side pocket.

"How about right now?"

He shook his head. "Meeting from eight thirty to nine. Loan association from nine to ten. Nothing after ten thirty."

I knew about the loan association. Kincaid lent out money, anything from a hundred bucks up, to various characters with new angles and approaches to old rackets.

If you've got a sucker on the hook and you need a couple of grand to rent a Caddy, a good apartment and some Brooks Brothers wardrobe for a front, Kincaid will underwrite you. He has no part in the caper himself, just a straight loan on a note. He operates on a standard ten per cent on most loans. Probably a lot more where the risk and profit run high. It's a perfect setup for a guy who wants to spread his money around where it gets a fast turnover without sticking his neck out.

"It's eight-thirty right now, Harry," I said. "I want upstairs before nine." I didn't put any hard stuff in it. You can't pressure the Harry's of the world.

He shrugged. "I don't write the schedule. I just read it."

"Then read it to Kincaid over the house phone and see if he can rewrite it. And while you're at it tell him why I'm here. He's got a boy named Hauptman working for him, a pock-marked kid who plays a lousy game of poker. Hauptman sent me a drop-dead note by phone. And he might be the man who shot up a hacky downtown about noon today. Maybe Kincaid doesn't know about that. Maybe this Hauptman is working a few angles of his own. I know that Pete tries to avoid the muscle stuff when he can."

"When he can," Harry said mildly.

"Right. But then there's this. Maybe Kincaid knew about that call. And maybe he knows about the shooting too. I was on my way to the Johns to tell them about both. I stopped here first. It's a courtesy call. But if he's too busy I'll go see maybe the Johns have time for me."

Harry listened quietly, licked his lips once when I was done and then walked away. I saw him pick up the house phone near the elevator, say a few words and then nod for me to follow him.

We got in the car and hummed up to the third floor. A pale, blond-haired kid in his twenties greeted us as the car opened. He was a very neat, clean gunman. But still a gunman. We stepped out into a large reception room. Upholstered benches lined the sides of the room and a huge photorama of Manhattan covered the rear wall. I've seen that same blow-up in half a dozen ad agencies and a few big magazines.

The blond kid nodded to Harry and then to me. "Loan association?"

Harry shook his head. That head of his saved him a lot of conversation. "Special session with Kincaid," he said. The kid nodded. He was studying to be a junior Harry.

We started toward the other end of the room, the one with the photorama covering the wall. It was a long walk. The upholstered benches were crowded with men, young men, old men, good dressers and flashy ones, cigar smokers and cigarette men. They were all talking at once, their voices probably a pitch or two higher than normal, their faces pinched and drawn into phony smiles. They were all as nervous as mother hens.

"He's a Texas oil man, see? Pig rich. Only he's got this yen to get his picture on a magazine cover. So I'll set up this dummy magazine office with two pretty dolls and an editor-type character, pencil behind his ear, horny-rimmed glasses, then we—"

"—now you know how the kids love to save those coupons. And the beauty part is that I've got the same printer who turns them out for this bubble gum company ready to make them for me. So it's not like counterfeit, it's the real thing. I could put fifty pushers out around the schools selling them for—"

"—and you sell it by radio. You buy up a hundred spot announcements on small stations and even give a money-back guarantee. All we say is it grows hair. We don't say nothing about how long it takes or what color hair or whose. All we say is it grows—"

"—three years I've been waiting for this chance. When I heard how her old lady goes in for this séance crap I knew this was fate beating down my door. I call myself Professor Miyako, the seventh son of a seventh son of the emperor of the cosmos. I need five G's for the right kind of equipment and rent money on this mansion over on Riverside Drive, then—"

The boys were all champing at the bit, each waiting his turn to whisper into Kincaid's rich ears. The smell of dirty money perfumed the atmosphere. Streetwalker's perfume.

We reached the far wall with its Manhattan photorama. Harry put one hand on the Empire State Building and pushed sideways. It was a sliding door. We stepped through it, out of the dirty money room and into a quiet office.

CHAPTER SEVEN

It was smaller than the reception room. The walls were papered with a black and silver stripe. The furniture was all in light woods and modern as the day after tomorrow. There was a desk that was shaped like an X-ray I once saw of my Uncle Ben's left kidney. Two book cases jutted out into the room from the walls. They were made of glass brick and pale blue light shone through them. A light gray carpet sponged under my shoes. It must have taken two men with vacuum cleaners four hours a day to suck dirt out of that pale gray.

I sat down in an armchair next to the desk. Harry pulled up an office chair alongside me and sat down. We waited maybe a minute. Then Kincaid entered from a side door. I saw a white-tiled bathroom behind the door as he stepped through and another door on the other side of the john. There was no end to this joint. If he told me he had a secret tunnel running from there to Hoboken, I'd have taken it without a blink.

Kincaid was tall and lean. He had a rawboned look. His suits were made to order and his shirts likewise. But they never seemed to completely cover his bony wrists or the inch of arm above them. He wore his hair long, brushed straight back, flat and black. A little like Abe Lincoln. More like a Midwest school teacher.

"Sorry about this mix-up, Boyd." He motioned me not to get up and stuck out his hand. I gave it a fair shake and he climbed around to the business side of his desk. "Harry told you how busy I am. Tuesday's a bad day for me. Every day is bad. Busy as a boarding-house john."

He offered me a cigar. I didn't reach. He tried with a cigarette and I figured I'd better take that or he'd run the scale through marijuana, hashish and opium. Harry stayed until Kincaid and I had lit up and then padded out through the reception room, probably stopping on his way to tell the businessmen they'd have to wait a while longer to see the big man.

"Okay," said Kincaid, after the door slid closed behind Harry, "you were never one for the long road home, Boyd. I figured if you pushed Harry to see me then it must have been important."

"Harry didn't tell you over the phone?" He said no. "Right. It's important, but more for you than me. You got a man named Hauptman on your payroll."

He squinted through cigarette smoke. "Could be."

"Not could be. Is. I tailed him here from a crummy barber shop that fronts for bookies, floating poker games and maybe a pimp or two. If he shuttles between there and here he's no customer. So he's on the payroll."

"So he is."

"So he put a knife in my back this morning—by telephone. You know about that?" He said nothing. "He wanted the address of a woman I mentioned in this morning's column."

"He's a ladies' man."

"He's a rat."

Kincaid closed his eyes for a moment and then opened them again. "I'll speak to him. Maybe he doesn't know you're on our VIP list. That's all?"

"That's not all. The guy who tipped me to this woman's address was a cabby by the name of Sam Baniff. I say was—he's dead now. A fat slug in the head, probably a .45. Only it tore a hole big as a Sunkist orange in his head, so I figure it was no ordinary shell. I think this bullet had an X carved into the lead the way some gunmen do to make it spread out when it hits. You know anybody who signs his bullets with an X?"

He shook his head. "Where's the tie to Hauptman?"

"He wanted the address. Sam had it."

"So he killed the only guy who could lead him to this cutie? That's bad strategy."

I smiled but not for the fun there was in it. "This Hauptman is no four-star general. His strategy stinks. I saw him try to switch the house rules in a poker game he's been playing with the same guys for a year now. Lots of guts. No brains."

"That's thin," he said. "To kill a guy who's going to talk against you, that's one thing. To kill a guy whose mouth you need, that's crazy."

"Then try it the other way. This woman has a husband. He's a blackmail artist. He's serving time in New Jersey for a bank job. When I heard that I knew somebody had cut a rotten cheese somewhere. Sam knew it too, and more. That slug stopped him." Kincaid sat quietly listening, nodding his bony face now and then. I scrubbed out the cigarette in an ashtray that must have measured a foot from end to end.

"So," I said, "maybe it's ass-backwards to kill a man

who's got the words you need. But it's straight center to kill one who's going to talk against you. Like you said."

"Like I said," Kincaid repeated. He ditched his butt alongside mine. He stared up at the ceiling for a minute. I folded my hands and waited for his play. "Hauptman didn't kill your man," he said. "He made the call, and a crummy job of it too. No reflection on your tail job, McGee." I nodded my thanks. "But the gunning, that's out."

"So we'll hold back on that for the minute," I said. "Now about that call."

"The call was from me, by way of Hauptman. I couldn't do it direct. It had to be fast and I don't like to push my friends."

"So you let other people do it for you?"

He shrugged. "This can be short because you know most of it already. When you smelled a rotten cheese over that bank job that Charlie Whipper pulled, your nose was putting you right. It was a frame-up."

"Meaning?"

"Meaning Whipper knows beans about bank heists—less. He walked past two bank dicks and stuck up the joint singlehanded without even a getaway car or a partner to take on the bank cops. He had on a red sport shirt and a plaid vest. He wanted to make sure they could spot him. And his gun was empty—M. T."

"So?"

"That's it. He wanted to make a jail and he made it, five years. You know why he wanted in? Because he had half a million dollars of other people's cash. He needed a safe place to hide his body. You know a safer place than a state pen?"

"Whose cash?"

Kincaid leaned back in his chair and put the tips of his fingers together like the church-steeple game we played when I was a kid. "He had a scheme, Whipper. It was right down his line—not bank jobs—blackmail. A very important man could be framed into saying some bad things before witnesses. Mister Important would pay a lot to buy back his words. Only Charlie needed some cash for operating expenses."

"The loan association," I said.

"Charlie came to me two years ago and laid out the game. He makes the contact, he handles the meeting, he collects the money. I keep way in back, where it's safe."

"Except for the investment," I said.

"Of course. These things take a little cash to set up. Fifteen hundred, that's all he said he needed. It came to three grand before we were done. But I fixed my interest rates on his take, not on his loan. The risk was high so the rates were high. Thirty-three and a third per cent of half a million is one hundred sixty-six thousand plus. That's how much he welched on."

"Let me run this down to check it," I said. "Charlie took some sucker for half a million. *Some* sucker! You underwrote the project for a one-third cut. That's a big piece of melon for a G loan."

"I got news for you," he said. "The First National Bank don't lend out money to Charlie Whipper."

"I know that," I said. "So he comes to you, the Last National Bank. You turn over the money. The deal goes through. But Charlie gets hungry. He wants the whole bundle."

"Tax-free," he said. I smiled.

"Charlie pulls the bank job before you can collect your share and he gets himself sent up for five years."

I stopped, pulled an ear and then threw the half-million-dollar question. "What happened to the cash?"

"His wife. Who else? She disappeared like a kid at the beach. She didn't even show up at his trial. I had every door in the courthouse covered. She didn't show any place, not even on radar. And that's two years now."

"Then came the dawn," I said. "Dawn today. My column hit the stand ..."

"I spotted Karen's name there and sent Hauptman out to scare the address from you. I underestimated you, Boyd."

"And I overestimated you, Pete. I never figured you for a gun job."

He frowned. "Hell, I said my boys didn't put the slug on Baniff. I know he was a personal friend of yours, McGee. I wouldn't pull that on you."

"Not for less than one hundred sixty-six thousand," I said. "Or is it the whole bundle you want now, Kincaid?"

"Just what's coming to me."

I thought it over for a minute and decided to give him one chance to square the deal. "Okay, you say Hauptman's gun is clean? Bring him in here, let him tell me that."

"Don't you trust me, Boyd?"

"Like you said, Baniff wasn't just a guy who worked for me. He was a buddy."

"Like I said." He reached under the desk and pressed a buzzer. The side door opened in a minute and Hauptman walked in.

"Made any good flushes lately?" I said.

His face paled. "This is the guy?" he asked Kincaid. "This is McGee? This is the guy from the barber shop.

He come in for a shave."

"Think again, Einstein," Kincaid said.

Hauptman made an effort and finally came up with it. "You tailed me," he howled, pointing a fat finger at me. His pock-marked face had the pained look of a man who'd been double-crossed.

"That's less than you did to Sam Baniff," I said.

"Did what to who?" he said. He played it as corny as a stock-company Hamlet. But that didn't prove he'd killed Sam.

"You put a .45 through a hacky on Forty-seventh Street at noon today," I said.

"Noon today I was at my brother-in-law's in Hoboken. His wife took sick with the croup and—"

"And you got nine witnesses to prove it," I said. "Well, look, Florence Nightingale, you weren't nursing your sick sister-in-law through palpitations, palsy or the pip. I was on the street corner when you came jockeying up behind Sam's cab and I saw your sweet puss on the right front seat of that Cadillac. And I'll swear to that on—" That was as far as I was prepared to lie. The only thing I could see when that Caddy went by was a green streak.

"You'll swear crap!" Hauptman roared. "With five men in a car going sixty-five or seventy you'll swear which one handled the gun?"

I relaxed with a smile. You can warn a dope about making breaks like that from now till New Year's. But get him under pressure, with the chair staring him in the face, and he'll fall right into the hole.

"There's your story," I said to Kincaid. "I'll bet bucks to buttons Hauptman handled the gun too. But it was one of your boys, no matter how you cut it."

Kincaid got up and came around the desk.

"Hauptman goes," he said. "We'll put him on a one-way train to L. A. and you'll never see his ugly kisser again." Hauptman scowled, showing me his ugly kisser. "That's all we can do there. I don't know which of the boys got trigger happy any more than you and they won't talk. Not even to me." I got up and buttoned my overcoat.

"But," he said, "we can do more in other places. Sure I'm out for the half-million, why not? Didn't Whipper try to take the whole bundle? So now we've got the shoe on the other foot. You give me Karen Lamain's address. I'll make it worth the trouble. Sooner or later I'll find it. I'd rather do it sooner."

"I like money," I said. "But you didn't hear me right, Kincaid. Sam was my buddy. I'm out for blood, not money."

I started for the door. Kincaid made one last bid. "But you'll take the cash if you can't get the corpse, no?"

Hauptman stepped in front of me, barring my way to the door. I feinted with my right hand, he ducked to the left. I booted him with my left foot. "I'll take the blood. That's all. I want Hauptman here and I don't care how I get him, by my own hand or in the chair at Sing Sing. Turn him over to the cops or kill him yourself or give him to me. That's up to you. I'll be home by four a.m. Let me know."

CHAPTER EIGHT

I walked out of Kincaid's office, my back set like there was a broomstick holding it up. I didn't expect any gun play there; Kincaid kept his place of business clean. But if there was going to be some slugs thrown I wanted to go with dignity. There were no bullets.

The kid on the elevator gave me his tip on the Hollywood divorce story. I jotted it down. My nerves were still popping from the meeting on the third floor, but I tried to concentrate on business. I still had a column to get out. I gave the kid a ten for the tip. It was worth more if it was an exclusive. But this kid didn't work for a very honest house so I could not count on that.

Out on the street a slight wind was blowing. I pulled up my collar and started back east. I had to walk back to my car and make a few more night spots before I could close the column for the night. I had to call the cab company and ask them to send a man over to deliver my copy to the paper, too. Sam wouldn't be waiting at my door at dawn anymore.

Past Third Avenue the streets were dark and empty now. They matched my mind. I tried to scare up a few thoughts but my brain was a scrap heap, a tired pile of junk that needed rest and fumigation.

Since noon I'd been walking around half empty inside. I moved because I had to, not because I knew just where I wanted to go or why. I was running on nerves and cigarettes. And the nerve supply was getting low.

I managed to put together two thoughts and even they weren't worth the try. I knew now that Kincaid's men had been responsible for Sam's death. That was thought number one. I also knew that I couldn't prove even to myself whether it was Hauptman or one of the others who did the actual gunning. What I'd said about that to Kincaid was pure bluff. That was thought number two.

I meant it about wanting to see Sam's killer as dead as Sam was now. But I knew damn well that I didn't have it in me to destroy five men, even four other Hauptmans, just to be certain I got my man. I had to know which one it was and know for sure. Then I'd go all the way.

I turned uptown at First Avenue. There was a dog on the street pulling his leash behind him and sniffing at the curb. That was the only living thing I saw. Somebody had been too lazy to walk him around the block on a windy night. I remember thinking then that lazy people shouldn't keep pets. Pets are a responsibility, like kids. And I remember thinking, after I'd passed the dog, that he was behind me, following me home. I turned around to send him on his way. It wasn't the dog behind me. It was Hauptman. Hauptman and his four friends.

He said, "That's him. See, he's got real pretty brown hair, like I said." And then he let me have it on the side of the head with something black and hard. Maybe it was the gun that killed Sam.

I didn't go down easy. I buckled at the knees and then pulled myself up, lurching to one side to avoid the gun again. I got in one right hand shot and a boot. Then the five of them were all over me.

Hauptman let me have it with the gun again. I went down on my knees. I was still fighting it. I never learn.

They took turns kicking me. I was still on my knees so they worked on my sides, the ribs, the shoulders, the arms. Then I folded up and they could get at me from the top. I got one in the ear and it whistled like the wind through telephone pole wires. After that I couldn't tell one from another. It was just a string of hard, pointed shoes running the length of my body. I held out as long as I could and then I gave them what they came for—Karen Lamain's address.

They kicked me in the head once more for a thank you. I passed out....

A drunk picked me up. I thought that was quite a switch. This dirty, foul-smelling man with eyes like fire and hands that shook picked me off the ground. I laughed. It was a loud, shrill laugh.

He said, "I know it. They come at you big as eagles with their sharp teeth. They'll gobble your head if you don't beat them off. I know it. But there's a doc down the street can fix you up with a powder. Or you can go to Bellevue, if you've got the stomach for it."

I let him help me up and then I stumbled off. I made it to the gutter and puked up the sandwich I'd had at the office. The drunk said, "I know it." I got away from him as fast as I could.

I made it to my car but it took a while. Then I just sat there sucking in air. I pushed fingers over my body and looked for broken things. But I couldn't tell the bent from the broken. I only knew that I was hurt. I didn't trust myself at the wheel. Not for any long driving. Not for as far as my apartment, three or four miles off. That seemed like from here to Chicago. I couldn't make that.

Something teased at my brain. I knew where I was, the East Sixties. Sutton Place was eight or ten blocks south. A girl named Maura Page lived at Sutton Place. I could make that.

I drove slowly, nursing the car down First Avenue. You could have walked faster than I was driving.... The ten blocks must have taken me ten or fifteen minutes. I was happy enough just getting there. Parking was another story. I knew enough not to try.

I pulled up in front of the door and let go on my horn. The doorman came out to see what was up. I paid a buck to get the car parked, but it was worth every red silk fiber in the bill.

Maura Page let out a shriek when she opened the door. I knew I didn't look like any Handsome Harry right then, but I didn't figure it was that bad. She couldn't even speak; she just waved me into the apartment.

There was a narrow foyer and then three steps down into the living room. The stairs had a banister. I used that. After that it was a cinch, just six feet of carpet to a sofa. I almost made it, too. But somewhere along the way I looked down.

I wasn't any taller than I'd been an hour before or ten years before that. But I might just as well have been looking off the Empire State Building. My shoes started swimming around beneath me and my legs were like stilts with six hinges. The hinges bent in all directions and I went down again.

When I came to, I was still on the floor but most of my clothes were gone. I had on my socks and underdrawers. There was something cold and wet wrapped around my forehead and everywhere I looked my body was covered with brown stains. Maura was working on my left leg with a bottle of iodine and a swab. That's what made the stain, the tincture of iodine. It stung like a rattler.

"You're up," she said.

"Second time tonight," I said. "The calendar says it's spring but tonight it's just fall, fall, fall."

She laughed and put the iodine bottle away. Then she went out and came back a minute later with a highball and a lit cigarette. The whiskey was the best.

I couldn't smoke without coughing so I gave her back the butt.

I told her a little about it. She didn't listen much. Instead she kept running her cool hand across my brow and repeating, "Shh, little boy, shhh."

I looked at my watch. It was nine-thirty. I should have been out working. But I couldn't have made it to the door. Her hand felt like ocean breezes and smelled like lilacs, with maybe a drop of iodine. I fell asleep twice and woke up each time, feeling the National Guard was charging after me. The first time it was nine thirty-five. The second time it was nine thirty-seven. She was there both times, which was nice. But there's no percentage in that kind of sleep.

She helped me up to the sofa and tucked a blanket around me. Then she brought some chicken broth. It was right out of one of Mr. Campbell's cans but it tasted like soup for the gods.

She turned on some soft music and sat down at the foot of the sofa. I finished two bowls of soup, half a box of wheat crackers and some Swiss cheese. We sat listening to the music while she hummed along and I munched cheese and crackers.

At ten o'clock there was a station break and five minutes of news. The usual stuff: some congressional committee was investigating the YMCA, a guy in Brooklyn had carved his girl up and hung himself, the French cabinet had fallen again.

I didn't pay much attention to that. I was looking at the walls of the room. There were paintings everywhere, big ones and little ones, fat ones and skinny ones. Some were of kids in Central Park, skating, sailing boats and wrestling in the grass. Some were of herself, in a paint-smeared smock, in an evening gown, in nothing at all. Most of them were of Mexicans.

There was a Mexican farmer and his family standing in front of an adobe. Nine kids, from an infant in arms to a boy taller than the father. There was another of the same family sitting inside the adobe eating beans and tortillas. Everyone was sitting on the floor.

There were a half-dozen more of other Mexicans, farmers, children, market women and with them were horses, dogs and bulls. They were good paintings, real, strong, full of color. It was like she had crammed a bright sun into her tubes of paint and just squirted it all over the canvases.

The news announcer droned on about a tenement fire in Harlem. I looked at the paintings of Mexicans with the poverty sticking out all over them. Only the way Maura painted them they didn't look poor, just strong. She probably made the same mistake a lot of rich people do. She probably thought it was fun to be poor.

"... Charles Whipper," the announcer said, and my mind came flying back from Mexico. "... he is believed to be armed. New Jersey prison authorities said that Whipper, serving five to ten years for armed robbery, made his escape at eight o'clock this evening with the aid of a prison laundry truck."

Good old Charlie. He must have heard that things were going too slow and quiet for me so he was coming on down to juice up the party.

"... The truck was found abandoned on Route Nine. A man answering Whipper's description stole a blue Buick, four-door sedan at approximately the same time. Whipper, a notorious blackmailer, was convicted of—"

I didn't need the rest of it. The announcer told me how Whipper had broken out; I knew the why and the where. The *why* was that Whipper had gotten his hands on a copy of my newspaper that afternoon and spotted the Karen Lamain item. He realized that Kincaid and his men would use that as a lead to Karen and the half million in cash. The *where* was easy: Whipper was on his way to Karen's Madison Avenue apartment.

And then I knew one other thing. The baby Charlie wrote about so lovingly, "How's our baby?" "Give my love to the baby"—that kid who wore no clothes, sucked no bottles and slept without crib or bed—I knew about that now too. "Baby" was a half-million in cash.

I reached out, switched off the radio and started to get up. Maura put two gentle hands against my chest and tried to hold me back.

"Let him come," she said. "Let them tear each other apart over the money. It's not your affair."

I pushed the soft hands aside and swung my feet off the sofa. "It *is* my affair, honey. The animal who killed Sam is my affair, with a capital 'aff'!"

I pulled on my clothes while my body screamed from every iodine patch. Maura walked around with a lit cigarette, flicking ashes on the floor, on chairs, on tables, snarling prettily, "Go ahead. Get your head broken. Get your teeth knocked out. Be a hero. Be a damn fool."

Her voice was crowded, choking, with frightened anger. I had nothing to say. I don't know how I felt about her right then. But suddenly I knew how she felt. She was falling in love with me in her own scared, crazy way. That was a lousy trick.

It was no good trying to explain things. If I could have explained what drove me all that day I would have told it to myself first. But there was no explaining.... At the door she tried once more. I put my mouth on hers and stopped the flow of words. She murmured something and my cheek came away wet where it touched her eyes. I pulled on my coat and hurried out.

The drive to Karen Lamain's place took five minutes. I had full control of things now. I hurt like hell but I knew what needed doing and I could get my body to do it pretty well. What it had to do right then was to take me to Charlie Whipper. Where Charlie was, Kincaid would be also. I wanted to see the two of them gun each other to death. I wanted to help a little.

Two blocks south of Karen Lamain's place I spotted the blue Buick, four door sedan with New Jersey license plates. Daddy had come home to "Baby."

I parked my car down the block from the house and looked around twice before getting out. I sidled my way up the rest of the block with my back to the wall of the building. I didn't want any stray dogs following me this time. I didn't want any stray shoes in the head.

There was nobody in the lobby of the building and the elevator was a self-service job. I rang for it and waited. It was on the third floor when I rang. Karen Lamain lived on the third floor. I watched the indicator hand move to the second floor and then to the letter L, for lobby.

I opened the door and walked into the car. I tripped over something. It was a man's body.

There was a hole in his back. I turned him over and saw the same hole in front. It was a small hole, a .30

caliber fired at close range straight through him. I recognized the face that stared up at me. It was Charlie Whipper. He died with his eyes wide open. He never had a chance to spend a penny of the cash he went to jail for. He died within spitting distance of his half-million dollar "Baby."

I stepped out of the elevator and closed the door in a hurry. I wasn't exactly buddy-buddy with the cops right then, and being caught in a self-service elevator with Whipper's dead body would not help my stock any.

I turned to go and two men walked quickly into the lobby. One of them wore a business suit. The other had on overalls and the printing across the front said, "Al's TV and Radio Service, 24 Hours a Day." The TV repairman had a tool kit in one hand and a huge television tube under his arm. I started to go.

The other guy was jabbering away and blocking my exit. "At least I think it's the picture tube. We keep getting these streaks across the screen. I called your partner earlier and he said—" I managed to get around them and I was halfway to the lobby door when they reached the elevator and opened the door. The guy who was jabbering away let out a shout.

"Stop that man! It's a murder!"

The TV repairman was at me in two steps. He tossed the little kit out of his hand and grabbed that twenty-one-inch tube with both fists. He lifted it way over his head and kept walking in on me.

"Make a move," he said. "Just one move, mister. This stuff blows up like a bomb."

CHAPTER NINE

The cops must have thought they had me over a barrel right from the start because they were rough—a lot rougher than the facts called for. So you could only figure that they were paying me back for my profession. I half expected that.

Most cops are afraid of only two things, politicians and newspapermen. A good newsman can build a rookie cop into a hero with a fat desk job in no time. He can do the reverse for a precinct captain if there's lots of personal hatred there. Cops know that and they respect the press because of it. But it's the kind of respect that lives far from Love Street. So once they've caught a newsman with a dirty nose it's shot-for-shot and he'd better cover up good in the clinches.

"Now look, McGee, we're not transcribing this yet. But let me warn you now—"

"—that you're putting it all down in your crowded little skull for future reference," I said. "That's not news, Lieutenant."

The room was small and dark. A single dim bulb in a ceiling fixture lit the gray walls and bare floor. There was a desk and chair at one end of the room and another chair at the other. In one, behind the desk, Captain Fallon sat, staring out of the window at the dark night. It was a revolving chair and it made a protesting squeal as he rocked it back and forth. I was in the other chair, a straight wooden affair. The freckle-faced lieutenant sat between us on a corner of the desk, his legs flung out into the middle of the room.

"I'll run it down again," Freckles said. He took a notebook from his pocket and flipped it open. The notes were stuff he had gotten from the radio car boys who arrived on the scene first. "Check me where I'm off.... You arrived at the Lamain apartment house at ten twenty-five. Before that, starting around nine, you spent the evening with a woman named Page, Maura Page, Sutton Place address."

I nodded and shifted in my chair. This was all the stuff I'd given to the radio car boys an hour before. I wondered how many more times I'd get it rammed down my throat before the night was out.

"Okay. Whipper was dead when you got here—it says. You were on your way to phone us when this man Winterley and the TV repairman walked in. Only in the excitement you completely forgot to tell Winterley and the TV man what was in the elevator." He looked up from the book and raised one eyebrow. I stared off into space, not moving a muscle. He went back to the book.

"You've got a couple of abrasions and lacerations along the face and hands and you admit a carload of black and blue marks around the ribs, stomach, chest and legs. Those you got at your gymnasium late today"—he looked up from the book again—"it also says here."

"At the gym," I said. "Right."

"You go there often?" he asked.

"Couple times a week."

"Hardly pays, does it?" he said dryly. It was more than just a joke, though. I started to say something but Captain Fallon cut me short. With his back still toward us he nodded his head, and I watched the reflection in the window pane. The background of the black night made the window an almost perfect mirror.

"Let's just get on with it," Fallon said. I shrugged.

"All right, McGee," Freckles said, "suppose you account for your time between noon today and ten-thirty tonight—all of it."

"Work, mostly," I said. "After you guys finished questioning me about Sam's murder I walked over to the office and put in a day's work. I left there around eight o'clock and made the rounds of a couple of night spots, getting some material for the column."

Freckles smirked. "What happened to the gym?"

"From three to four," I said. "I like to break around three for some push-ups, knee bends and a massage, like some guys break for coffee or a drink. The gym is on the top floor of the office. Check with Johnny, the gym attendant."

Freckles nodded and made a note of it. Fallon shook his head at the window, still not bothering to turn back to us. "No dice," he said. "If this Johnny guy sees you twice a week for years he'd never remember if it was yesterday or today or last week when he saw you."

I made like I was thinking that one over and then said, "Probably right, Captain."

"Thanks," Freckles said, but it's not the word he meant. "Okay, so let's quit the clowning. You admit your normal procedure is to make the nightclubs till three in the morning. How come you quit at nine tonight?"

"Dull night, Lieutenant. Nothing doing."

He didn't buy that, he just skipped over it. "Let's get this Maura Page on the record. Who is she?"

"My third cousin on my mother's side, from Brooklyn, about twenty-three years old, size thirty-eight bust, red hair, lips you love to bite, mole on her left—"

"We're not interested in your hobbies," Freckles said. "Where does she fit in?"

"She serves up some fine hot broth and wheat crackers at nine o'clock at night. That's better than you can do at most night clubs."

"Maybe she served you a couple of clouts in the kisser, too?" He laughed. "I'd sooner believe that than this gymnasium routine you've been giving us."

"So you believe that because you've got a swamp for a mind, and I'll believe the gym routine because it's true and Captain Fallon there gets to go home early. Is it a deal?"

Freckles blew his cork. "Now cut the crap, McGee. You were the first man on the scene of two killings committed within ten hours of each other. You think that's a comedy? You think we're a bunch of burlesque stooges come to set up the laughs for you? You think we're fools?" I didn't answer that one. You can get thrown in the can for answering that kind of question honestly.

"All right," he snarled. "Then read it down once more. And this time skip the fancy part about the gym and give us some details about those cuts on your face and this Page dame—lots of details."

"It still reads the same," I said. "Truth is like Republicans. It never changes."

That tore it. He sat on the corner of the desk, clenching and unclenching his fists while twin coals of anger glowed from his eyes. I figured he'd reach out and clout me one for sure. I wouldn't have minded that. When you can get them to use their hands they forget their brains some place.

Fallon swung around in his chair and brought his

hand down on the desk with a loud, splatting sound. "Cut it!" The tension held for one more moment and then Freckles opened his fists and I slumped back into my chair. "All right," Fallon said, "now tell him what's on your mind, Pete. He won't know what to answer till you let him know how far you're ready to go on this."

Freckles nodded, wiped his palms on the thighs of his trousers and took a deep breath. "McGee, we don't generally work morning and night, you know. They yanked us out of bed when Whipper was reported shot. They knew the captain and I were working on something around Whipper so they—"

"Boil it down, Pete," Fallon said. He swung back around in the chair and went back to staring out of the window.

A quiet little smile dribbled down from the corners of Freckles' mouth. He looked like a man preparing to cut into a thick slab of steak. He was going to get one hell of a kick out of this, whatever it was....

"McGee, twelve o'clock today a hacky named Baniff was shot up. Baniff was your best friend. He was on his way to tell you something about Whipper—you admit that much. The Whip couldn't stop him from prison, but some boys working for Whipper on the outside could do it for him. Now if you figured it that way you'd be out gunning for them—for the guys who killed your pal. Only tonight you heard that Whipper himself was on the loose. So what could be better than gunning the guy behind Baniff's murder? McGee, you killed Whipper."

He was up from the desk and across the room in three steps. He threw the door open wide and shouted out into the hall. "Lee!" Fallon swung back around in his chair. A uniformed cop stuck his head through the open door.

Fallon shook his head. "Skip it, Lee," he said. The cop looked around the room once and then pulled his head back out. "Close the door, Pete," Fallon said. Freckles closed the door without a word. He was silently wishing the captain would drop dead. You didn't need a swami to read his mind.

Fallon leaned across the desk toward me. "Let's play this friendly, Boyd. You're no professional troublemaker, like some of the news men. Fred Henrich tells me you're a square shooter. I'll go along with a square shooter—newspaperman or not."

Fred was my man at headquarters, the one they broke for locking up the councilman's son-in-law. "Thanks, Cap," I said. "But I'm being square as far as I know how. You boys are on a spot"—Freckles threw me a dirty look—"I know that much. And I've got a pretty good idea of where the pressure is coming from. But all I asked for was time to play this thing my way and deliver Sam's killer to you in a sack. Now, if you'll just—"

"More time?" the lieutenant asked. "You want more time? Maybe time to kill a few more people? Maybe time to make the department look like a pack of chumps for doing business with a crazy man killing for revenge?"

Fallon shook his head. "Drop it, Pete." He turned to me. "We gave you what you asked for, Boyd. We went along as far as we could. But Whipper's breaking out of stir and now this—it makes things tough for us. Sure, we're the cops, but we can't write our own ticket all the way. We've got a mayor to account to. And he's got a city council and the governor to account to. And then there's the newspapers. *Especially* the press boys. They eat this stuff up." You could tell that the captain had a deep love for the press boys.

It was a straight appeal. The guy was trying to do a job and he needed a hand in it. Besides which, Freckles was ready to make whatever trouble he could if the captain's friendly policy didn't work so well. And while I knew I could outthink Freckles with one brain tied behind my back, I didn't want to take the time for it. I couldn't afford it.

"Okay," I said, kind of low. "Hold the press boys off. Just give me a thirty-minute start before you break the story and I'll give you whatever I've got. But I've got to have that much time to knock out a couple of paragraphs for my column explaining my side of things. Otherwise the competition will cut me to confetti before I've got one hand up."

Freckles didn't even take time out to think it over. "No soap," he growled.

"Shut up," Fallon said. The captain did take the time for it.

Freckles leaned over the desk. "Captain, we can't make a deal with McGee. You know how the papers feel about the department giving out exclusive stories. They'll put it to us for sure. McGee is just one paper. There are five more in this town."

That decided Fallon, that part with the threat in it. That's the way a mind like Fallon's works and Freckles hadn't learned that much yet. "To hell with the press," Fallon said. "McGee is a material witness, not a newsie. When publishers start running the department, I'll turn in my shield. Now let's get this thing started."

It was my round but Freckles figured the fight wasn't

over yet. He had a few more punches left to throw. He told me that with one thin smile.

Freckles left the room in search of a police stenographer and Fallon swung around to stare out of the window some more. I took that time to get my story straight. The gym routine was out. I'd give them the whole line on Kincaid and his boys, including the part where they bashed my skin in from top to bottom. One of them killed Sam and I'd have been a happier man if I could have evened the score with my own hands. But you can't have everything.

The part about Karen Lamain bothered me. I didn't have to hold back on her, now that Whipper was dead. But once the newspapers got a hold of her role in the case they'd dig back to that item I ran about her and Kingsley Benson. And with his wife's million-dollar divorce suit pending it would be rough on Kingsley B.

Funny about that. That item Sam gave me about Benson and Karen Lamain had dragged me into the whole bloody mess. Now Sam was dead and Whipper was dead, but Kingsley Benson was still on the spot. And Calvin was there with him. Poor little rich muddle-headed Calvin. He probably still thought I planted that item in the column just to put the skids to Benson, Calvin and his whole damn law firm.

So, while Freckles was getting things set up for my deposition, I decided to do Calvin and his client a good turn by steering the spotlight away from Karen Lamain. That way I might be able to keep it from splashing over onto Kingsley Benson. Which was okay with me so long as it didn't cost me anything.

That's the way I told the story to the stenographer. I couldn't drop Karen Lamain from it completely since she was the wife of one of the corpses. But I just touched on her lightly, omitting the part about having been at her place earlier in the day and details on the microphones, amplifiers and other stuff I uncovered there. I figured Fallon's men had given her place a good going-over by then. They didn't need any more help on that score. What I didn't know was how good a going-over they'd given it.

When I got to the part about Kincaid's men roughing me up, Freckles smiled happily. It proved that he was right for suspecting that gym story. Maybe he smiled too because he liked the image of Hauptman and the others pulping my brains. Anyway, he was a happier police lieutenant when it was over.

The stenog went out to type up my notes and we sat around smoking. About twenty minutes later the stenog returned with typed copies and we read them. Freckles took out a pen and handed it to me with a mile-wide grin. He was too happy. I examined both ends of the pen to make sure it wouldn't explode in my hands. I shrugged and signed the paper.

Freckles took the paper from me and waved it at the air several times to dry it. I lit another cigarette.

"Well, gentlemen," I said, "it's been more fun than the zoo. But I've got a deadline to meet. I'll move along now."

Freckles stopped waving the paper, stared at my signature and smiled. "What's your hurry, McGee? You've got all the time in the world." I made like I didn't hear the rusty note in his voice. I turned to go.

"Lots of time," Freckles said. I started for the door. "Maybe even years," he said. I put my hand on the knob and turned it. "McGee, you're a perjurer and you're under arrest."

I whipped around to face him. Freckles wasn't

smiling now. Fallon was still staring out at the dark. He was either in on this from the start or was willing to go along with it. Either way he wasn't going to fight Freckles on it.

"What the hell kind of perjury?" I said.

"Tell him, Captain," Freckles said. Lieutenant Freckles was giving orders now. Fallon swung his chair around, ran a finger under his damp collar, closed his eyes for a second and then opened them again.

"We got a report tonight," he said. It was like a frog croaking. He cleared his throat; "We got a report just after we came back with you tonight, McGee. A report on Karen Lamain's apartment. She wasn't there after Whipper was killed. We didn't think she would be. We had the laboratory guys go over the rooms. They found five good specimens of your prints all over the place. You swore you were never in Karen Lamain's place. That's why the lieutenant is charging you with perjury."

It was a pretty cheap little frame-up. Not that they forged the prints or anything. They didn't have to. I was in Karen's apartment and I denied it. But it was a cheap frame anyway.

Freckles knew I wasn't holding out to help myself. Maybe he knew I was doing Kingsley Benson a favor to repay him for what that item in my column had cost him. Maybe he didn't. But he knew I was doing it to help somebody besides myself. So why not tip me off that they've found my prints in the Lamain apartment and give me a chance to save my own hide before signing? Why not? Because Freckles wanted me right where he had me. Over a big, brown barrel.

"Okay," I said. "There's a slight error in the statement

and I'm ready to revise it."

"Slight!" Freckles laughed. "It's a hole as big as your feet. That ain't slight, McGee."

"Right," I said. I was ready to eat crow. It was late. I had work to do, sleep to get and breakfast to eat. Also I had plans for the next five or ten years. Plans that didn't include wearing striped suits and numbers. "Right you are, it's a big error. But big or small, I'm willing to straighten it out."

Freckles thought about it a minute. Fallon nodded. The captain was back in command. "Okay," the lieutenant said. "We might make a deal. Provided you give it to us straight about Karen Lamain."

I gave it to them as straight as an Ohio highway, everything about searching her apartment, finding the mikes and equipment, the letters from Whipper, everything. The idea that I could save Calvin and his client by holding back what I knew about Karen Lamain was just dandy until it meant fighting a perjury rap. Then it was strictly a matter of survival of the nearest. And I was as near and dear to Boyd McGee as anything could get.

I gave them the story once and then waited for them to make me run it down a second time for the stenog. They didn't ask me for that. They weren't satisfied with the text yet.

"Let's try it once more," Freckles said. "And this time let's get in some stuff about the money and Karen Lamain's whereabouts." He lit a cigarette and sneered through the smoke. Then he turned on a bright light and beamed it at me. It was the first time they stooped to that kind of crap.

I put up one hand to shield me from the light and peered out at Freckles' shadowy figure. "What money?"

I asked. I knew what money. But all of a sudden this wasn't such a friendly session and I was beginning to get my hackles up.

"The half million, wise guy. The dough that Karen Lamain took with her when she lammed out of her place tonight. Give."

I gave up trying to shield off the light and closed my eyes instead. "Half million? Dollars?"

He snorted through the darkness. "Not seashells. Now give."

I turned away from the light and opened my eyes. He leaned over and pulled me into the light again. I put my hand back over my eyes. "That's a lot of money," I said.

He moved into the circle of light and stuck one thick finger under my nose. "At noon you didn't know anything about Sam Baniff's murder. Tonight you know all about it. You never saw Karen Lamain's apartment up to five minutes ago. Now you know it from A to Z. Okay, we think you're holding out on the dough and her hideout too. You got three seconds to get your memory back."

I took a drag on my cigarette and blew a smoke ring up at the light. "One," he whispered.

I flicked ashes from my knee. "Two," he said, louder now.

I dropped the cigarette on the floor and ground it out with my heel, "Three," he roared. I crossed my arms and settled back in the chair. There was a moment of silence. Then he dipped into the bright circle of light again and grabbed me by the lapels. He yanked me out of the chair and I hung there, limp, not making a move in defense.

"We've been too easy," he said. "We babied you

because you're the press. Well, the gloves are off now." He lifted one fist and pulled back on me. I didn't move.

"Try it," I said. "Just one, that's all. Maybe I'll serve a year or two for perjury or maybe not. But you'll be patrolling the garbage dumps of Brooklyn for the rest of your rotten life, I swear. So go ahead, just once. I'll love it."

The bright light etched deep shadows into his ugly face. Lines of confusion twisted in and out, over his brow and around his mouth. Then he let out a blast of air and dropped me back into the chair. "Lee!" he roared. The uniformed cop came through the door. Freckles turned and walked out the same door.

"Lock him up and throw away the key," he snarled over his shoulder.

CHAPTER TEN

Lee took me out to the desk sergeant. I turned in my wallet, keys and other junk and the sergeant put me on the blotter. When they got to the part about the specific charge the sergeant came around the desk and held a whispered conference with Lee. They kept that up for two or three minutes while I studied the spots on the walls. Then Lee hotfooted it back to the other room to consult Freckles and the captain. He came back a minute later and they entered a charge of disorderly conduct. The boys were getting chicken.

I took that as my cue and started kicking up another stink. I threatened the pack of them with false arrest, violation of constitutional rights, intimidation and six other things. It didn't work. If they want to hold you bad enough they'll throw that D.C. at you and everyman-cop of them will swear he saw you pull a knife or make like you were going to. You can't win against that kind of a deck.

They gave me an empty cell with a washstand, two beds, a piece of soap and a towel. It wasn't much worse than some hotels I've booked. Only the room service was pretty feeble; there wasn't a Scotch and water in the house and they kept the key.

I stretched out on one of the cots and chain smoked, scraping out the butts on the floor and lining them up in a neat row below the cot. I thought about what the cops were after. They wanted to know about a half million dollars that Karen Lamain was supposed to have. That figured to be the same money that her old man had blackmailed a couple of years before—the half million that Pete Kincaid was after. Kincaid's boys had beaten me just this side of the grave for it. The cops jugged me for it. It was a very important half million. But then I don't know any that isn't.

I knew what Kincaid was after. He didn't have to tell me or get five of his boys to beat it into me. Take any minute of any day in the life of a man like Kincaid and ask yourself what he's after and then answer, money, every time. If you're wrong once in a thousand, I'll eat it.

But with the cops there was another wheel turning. This half million had been squeezed out by Whipper more than two years earlier, just before he pulled the phony bank job that gave him a cozy cell in the Jersey pen, far from Kincaid's gunmen. In those two years not a line had appeared in the press. And keeping a half-million-dollar extortion out of the headlines is like keeping a lawyer's mouth shut. It can't be done.

I've known the cops to hold out on the press for six

or seven days, in cases like murder or jewel theft where they figure it for an inside job and don't want to scare off their number one suspect. Once, in a kidnapping case, they held out for two weeks, hoping to save the victim's life by not exposing things too early. It didn't help.

That's what impressed me, this two years of total secrecy. Once the local Johns send out a national police alarm the lid is off. With every hick sheriff and two-bit constable in on the play, you've got as much secrecy as a network radio show. The only way you can command the kind of silence they kept around that half million is to keep the thing in a two- or three-man conference room. And that way you can't recover your half million. Which meant that the money was strictly second target. Okay. But what in God's little world was target number one?

It had something to do with the scrub-heads, the two Harvard boys who played rough before breakfast. From the start I figured it was those two who were squeezing Captain Fallon. But they acted more like a couple of school kids playing copper or a pair of state income tax clerks out to put some thrills in a dull job. They were raw, crude and stupid. The governor must have been all that and more, because it figured now. They were the governor's boys all right and they had the city cops jumping through hoops.

That's why I was in that jail cell. A department full of Johns were trying to get the governor's men off their necks by offering me up as a sacrifice. The governor gets me and the cops get to go back to their pinochle game. I ran a little routine item about a tobacco tycoon who was loving it up with some convict's wife and Captain Fallon and his men were using that to tie me in with Karen Lamain and the blackmail money and more. Now I knew where I was sitting. The only thing I didn't know was how to get off.

The cops didn't want me for Whipper's killing. That was so much talk. They didn't want to hold me for perjury either. All they wanted was to hold me long enough for the governor's boys to get down there and pick me up. After that the city cops could wash their hands of it. But I couldn't. I was the patsy.

That thought brought me off the cot. I began pacing the cell. I wanted out. But a habeas corpus wouldn't do it. If they had to, the Johns could drop that disorderly conduct charge and switch it to perjury. They had me there. It was only a technicality, but lots of men have died because of technicalities.

What I needed right then was bail. It was four-thirty in the morning and court didn't convene until ten. No judge, no bail. So I sat back down again, lit a fresh cigarette from the old one and scrubbed that one out in a line with the rest. I'd never have enough cigarettes to last me until ten.

Then something else started bothering me—the column. In ten years, I'd never missed a deadline. There was an emergency copy of the column, full of old jokes and anecdotes, lying in my file at the office. The idea was to run that in the event of delay, disease or drunkenness. But in ten years they'd never had to pull that one out of the files. And now, in half an hour, they'd be setting it into type. And somehow that hurt more than anything else.

Sounds crazy, doesn't it? But did you ever get a medal for never being late to class or a gold watch for twenty-five years of faithful service or just have one of your pals say, "Good old Al, he's always there in the pinch"? Okay, then you know how it feels.

After that I just lay there staring at my watch and thinking about it. It was four thirty-five now. In another five minutes the column should have been completed …

It was four-forty now. The copy should have been on its way uptown to the press room.... Harlow, my editor, would be waiting to give it the final eye for libel loopholes and such.... The guys at the teletype would be getting ready to bang it out over the wires to the syndicate. One hundred and six other papers were waiting for it around the country. And I was just waiting … waiting … waiting. Fifteen minutes to press time.

Lee, the uniformed cop, came around then to peer in through the bars. I was in no mood for happy talk. I rolled over on my belly and turned my face to the wall.

"McGee," he said.

"Scram," I said.

"Don't play it so tough," he said.

"Go away and let me die," I said.

"You sick?" His voice held anxiety.

I rolled back over and lifted my head from the mattress. "Yeah. I'm dying from a strange South American fever carried by prison cots. It's called the crud. Scram before I give it to you."

He laughed. "I've had it," he said.

I flopped my head back on the pillow. "You look it," I said.

"You want out?" he asked.

So now they were playing it that way. I turned my head back to the wall. "Fade," I said. "I'm as clean as a babe. But you boys couldn't get me to talk with a mallet and chisel."

He laughed. *He* thought it was funny.

"It's no deal. I'm not making you a deal. I'm saying you're sprung, off the hook, free like the birdies."

I turned back slowly, hoping he wouldn't go up in smoke, hoping he wasn't a convict's dream. He was still there. I rolled off the bed and walked very carefully to the cell bars. "Say it again. But make it simple. Just say, 'Go.'"

"Go." He stuck a key in the lock and the door sprung open. "It's right down the hall. There's a couple of gentlemen waiting to see you."

I was halfway out the door when he said it. I stopped there and backed into the cell. "Two of them?"

"Three." To him a couple was three.

I nodded. "Two of them with real white shirts, thin neckties and short haircuts?"

He smiled. "And another," he said. "Older, heavy, like a lawyer or a businessman." The scrub-heads. The governor's boys. And with reinforcements.

"I don't want it," I said. "Tell them I voted for the governor last term but I'll vote straight Anarchist before I do it again."

He laughed again. "Either way, the deal goes," he said. "You can talk to them or not, but the charge is dropped."

I closed one eye and examined him with the other. He didn't look like he was taking the needle, or smoking the weed, or swallowing Benzedrine and sweet wine. So I went along with it.

We walked down the corridor to the same room where Fallon and his lieutenant had questioned me. They were gone now. It was just like Lee had said, the two scrub-heads and a third guy who looked like a lawyer or business man. He wasn't either. I knew him from three elections back. It was the lieutenant governor.

I whistled, long and low. "They flew you down here for this?" The lieutenant governor motioned me to a chair and smiled. "Skip it," I said. "I'm impressed, Mr. Colombo, but the story stays the same. I don't know anything about Karen Lamain or the half million or who killed Cock Robin or anything."

He laughed, warmly. It wasn't phony either. "We're aware of that, McGee. This whole thing's been a botch from the start. I'm here to straighten things out."

I sat down. "You I'll vote for," I said.

"Watch him," one of the scrub-heads said. "He's got a tongue like quicksilver, Mr. Colombo." That was Sloan, the blond-haired kid with the watery gray eyes. That was the boy who'd slapped, punched and kicked me silly while his partner held a gun on me. I loved them both.

"That will do, Sloan," Lieutenant Governor Colombo snapped. He was friendly, all right. But he had a punch when he needed it. "You'll have to excuse these boys," he said to me. "They're new. They never should have been assigned to contact you. But it was all done so quickly the morning your column appeared that I never had a chance to okay the orders." I nodded silently. "They're right out of training school," he said. "But they mean well."

"So does a momma eagle, but she'll kill you just the same."

He nodded. "I'm not excusing them," he said.

"Just so long as that's understood. Because before this dance is through I'm going to have a piece of his hide." I shot out my left hand and pointed at Sloan. The shirt cuff slid back and exposed my wrist watch. It was five minutes to five. "Look," I said. "I know you for a reasonable man, Mr. Colombo. If there's something I can do for you let me know and I'll consider it. Anything reasonable, that is. But I want two things from you first. First, I want fifteen minutes with a telephone. I've got maybe three or four minutes to go before press time. If I can get to a phone they'll hold the presses and let me read in some stuff."

"Right," he said. I got up and started out of the room. He coughed once. "But first there's something else. There's something you can do in your column as part of the bargain."

I turned back. "There isn't much time," I said.

He walked in toward me and lowered his voice. "I can put it in one minute. You must know at least half already, maybe more."

"Shoot."

"You know that Whipper had himself jailed to evade some men who were in on that blackmail job with him."

"Kincaid," I said. "Anybody else?"

"No, just Kincaid. The others were his hirelings. Only we didn't know it was Kincaid until last night. You did that for us." He nodded his thanks and I waved it off. "What you don't know is who was being blackmailed and how it was done. The victim was Governor Bellows."

That didn't stir the hair on my head. I figured it was the governor or somebody damn close to him. And that explained why Whipper had himself chucked into a Jersey pen instead of one in his home state where the governor would have him under his thumb.... Colombo nodded and motioned again for me to sit. I didn't. He started talking.

"Two and a half years ago, just before the election, Governor Bellows held an investigation of the rackets on New York City docks. The governor's political opponents were attempting to beat him at the polls by claiming that he had been too lenient with the dock racketeers. The governor called some of the longshore leaders up to Albany and personally interrogated them. Everything pointed to one man, a big-time thug named Langley."

I nodded. I remembered the investigation. I remembered Burt Langley. Who didn't? He was the strong arm of New York's waterfront. "The trouble was," Colombo continued, "Langley had disappeared. We swore out a subpoena and tried every way to apprehend him. But he had vanished completely.

"Then, unknown to any of us, Governor Bellows was personally contacted by this man Whipper. Langley wanted a private conference with the governor, Whipper said. The governor checked into Whipper and found that he actually had worked with Langley at one time and that the two were quite close.

"The whole thing seemed plausible to Governor Bellows. He didn't like the idea of a secret conference. But the election was drawing near and the papers were making things hot for us. And so, without mentioning it to anyone, Governor Bellows agreed to meet with this man, Whipper, and Langley. They met at a hotel on Times Square."

I smiled. I remembered that hotel from a time when I went there to collect a blackmail photograph for my actor friend. Whipper must have held all his business conferences there.

"I say *they* met," Colombo continued. "Actually, only Whipper and two others were present. Langley was not. Whipper explained that Langley would not show up for the first conference until he was convinced that the governor would not attempt to have him arrested there and then. That too seemed part of the gangster pattern to the governor and he accepted it. I can only say now that the urgency of the situation and the personal pressure placed upon the governor as leader of the party was responsible for his readiness to accept the situation."

I grunted my understanding. But I could almost tell what was coming and I saw that the governor had been a first-rate chump.

Colombo wiped the corners of his mouth with thumb and forefinger and started in again. "With the others present, Whipper outlined the conditions under which Langley would agree to a public inquiry. The conditions were, of course, preposterous. But knowing the situation, you can see that the governor was anxious to close with this Langley. He felt that once he could confront Langley personally he would be able to handle the rascal. The governor, as you know, was a fine attorney in his own right at one time."

Some attorney. He had agreed himself right into a blackmail squeeze. But there's a lot a sensible guy will do when the walls are closing in on him. "Let me cut through this for you," I said. I didn't want to rush the man, but minutes were being wasted by the handful. "The governor agreed to all the conditions. He wanted to get his hands on Langley before the elections and he was willing to swallow a lot to do it."

"Not quite," he demurred.

"But awful close," I said. "So he talked himself right

onto a spot. Because what the governor didn't know was that Whipper no more represented Langley than he did the Boy Scouts or the Young Women's League. Whipper just represented himself. And those two characters he brought along weren't window dressing. Whipper had gotten the governor to compromise himself right before the election and in front of two witnesses."

The lieutenant governor sighed. "That's about it. Whipper could have sold that kind of evidence to the opposition for—well, he could have named his own price. And the price was half a million dollars."

"Who got stung for it, the party?"

"The governor, personally. He refused to pass on the responsibility for his own errors to the rest of us. He sold every bit of stock and property he owned. It all but broke him."

It was a very sad story. But I wasn't crying for Governor Bellows. I was saving my tears for Boyd McGee—he might need them. "So?"

"McGee, we're determined to smash this thing once and for all. This Lamain woman has the money and more than that. You see, she was one of the two others present when Governor Bellows made the agreement. The other man is dead, over a year now. Alcoholism."

"You want Karen Lamain, right?"

"Right. The money is not important, except as evidence, of course."

"Of course," I said, but not very firmly. I'd like to live to the day when a half million isn't important. Even to an honest politician.

"You can lead us to her," he said.

"How?"

The two scrub-heads had been as quiet as the desert

up to then. Now they hopped into action. Sloan, the gray-eyed blond, swung in first. "You know how, McGee. This Lamain dame is on the run. She didn't even bother to pack her clothes. All she took was the money. And now she's out there some place." He pointed out the door to the rest of the city.

Taylor jumped in then. He was the orator. He was also the boy who held the gun while Sloan massaged me.

"Out there alone," he said, "scared witless. Nobody to turn to. Running from the cops and running from Kincaid's men. She needs help. She's desperate. So she turns to your column. She knows you're involved in this but she doesn't know whose side you're on—Kincaid's, the cops, or maybe your own. But she's plucking at straws."

"And there," Sloan joined in, "there in your column, just when all seems lost, she finds help."

A great performance. They could have filmed it on the spot, and stuck it in five hundred theaters around the country and nobody would have known the difference between that and most of the crap Hollywood offers up.

I ignored the movieland twins and turned back to Colombo. "That's what you want? You want me to run a teaser in my column? Something that will suck her in?"

Colombo started to answer but Taylor got there first. "The same kind of trap her old man used on the governor," he said. "Poetic justice. And you're the man who can make it possible."

I looked at my watch. Time was running out on me. I wanted to cut the deal a little finer but the clock wouldn't let me. So I decided to put in with them.

Only Sloan didn't like my hesitation. He came up behind me just the way he had the morning before when Taylor held the gun.

"Cut the crap," he snapped. "You know you've got to go along with us, so quit stalling." I looked at him once, hard, and then turned to Colombo.

"I said there were two conditions. One was the telephone call."

Colombo smiled. "And the other?"

"This." I whipped around, pulled my fist back at waist level and shot it into Sloan's lean frame. He didn't have any fat but my fist sank into guts two inches deep. He doubled over and sank to the floor holding his belly. The others didn't move. When I left he was holding himself up on one elbow and a knee and retching out his last meal. Taylor was purring over him like a mother.

Colombo growled, "He deserved it, the young fool. The idiot. He nearly threw the whole thing back in the pot."

I got my editor on the phone. First, he checked to make sure I was still alive. Then he told me to drop dead. I didn't argue much. He had good reason to be churned up. He was as much responsible for my deadline as I. He had to answer to the publisher. And newspaper publishers don't joke about missed deadlines. On a newspaper staff you're better off dead than late.

I gave him the item I'd picked up from the elevator operator at Kincaid's and a few others I had in my notebook. Then I tried to recall four stories that were nesting at home in my hold file for release that morning. I recalled three verbatim and had to let the other one go. Then I went back over the whole column and dropped in three teasers, one as a lead, one near the middle and one at the end.

The first one ran: “K. L., call me, I can help you.” The one near the middle read, “K. L., don’t worry about K., we’ll protect you.” That was in case she figured Kincaid would get to her before we could. The last one said, “K. L., the money is yours. We can make a deal with the guy who got squeezed.” The only thing left to offer her was the moon. And I would have too, if she’d been the romantic type.

About those teasers. If you use them just as direct communication, a way to save on postage stamps, the editor won’t like it. But if you keep them interesting, so that you’ve got the public with its tongue hanging out, it doesn’t hurt your sales any. And if you can break a real story around it the next day or so, *then* you’ve got something. That’s what I hoped I had—something.

I got back my wallet, keys and the rest from the desk sergeant. He opened the record book for me and showed me a blank space where my name had been. I don’t know how they do that. Those pages are supposed to be numbered so that you can’t tear one out and a dash of ink remover will make a smear you can see from across the room. I’ve seen it done before and I still don’t get it. But it was my name they were clearing so I didn’t say a mumbling word.

Outside it was still pitch black. But if you turned to the east you could see the faintest gray streaks coming up over the horizon. I stood on the steps of the jailhouse and the spring night air felt good against my face. My back hurt and my body was beginning to remember that it had taken too much punishment for one year, let alone a day. I took in a deep breath and headed north for home.

CHAPTER ELEVEN

My car was parked outside of Karen Lamain's apartment house where I'd left it seven hours earlier, so I kept an eye peeled for a taxi. There aren't many cabs on the street at dawn and most of them hang around midtown, near the hotels and all-night cafeterias. Damn few of them stick around the Centre Street jailhouse. Not much taxi trade comes out of there. Mostly the paddy wagon crowd. I had to settle for the subway.

I've only got one thing against the subway—everything. It's noisy, they keep it like a home for untended pigs and it stinks. I figure they should either give everybody a helicopter and use the underground passages for growing mushrooms or else clean up the joint. And don't think I hate it just because I've got enough cash to own a convertible. I've stayed out of subways since before I had enough money to make a down payment on a package of Chiclets.

I found an empty bench in the subway station and sat down to wait for a train. That's another thing that I love about subways. New York is supposed to be a town that bustles right around the clock. But you could grow a beard waiting for a train after two in the morning. There are two things you can do then, sleep or think. I thought.

I thought about Karen Lamain taking a powder. The cops and the governor's boys took it for granted that she pulled out after Whipper was killed. Maybe they even figured she had gunned him. There was motive enough. After tending Whipper's money all the time he was up the river maybe Karen got to feeling like it was all hers. And when Charlie broke out of jail, maybe she decided that half a million was better than half of a half. And maybe she shot him. Maybe.

Personally I didn't lean toward that. First off, if she killed him in the elevator he was either coming up to her place or going out. So why not wait till he got there or get him before he left? Why take the chance of being caught in a public elevator with a dead man and a gun in your hand?

Secondly, there was that gun. There wasn't any gun in her apartment when I searched it. Sure, it could have been with her at the time, in her handbag. It was a small gun, judging by the size of the hole in Whipper's back. But why would she have the gun with her the morning I searched her place—before there was any reason to think that Kincaid was about to discover her hideout? It could be that she carried the gun with her from the day Whipper was sent up. It could be that she was permanently scared. But that didn't fit the pattern.

Kincaid's restaurant-gambling house-and-what-not was on Fifty-eighth Street and Lexington. Karen's apartment was just twelve blocks from there. She knew that in a city as big and unfriendly as New York you could live two doors down from a guy whose sister you defiled—like it says in the magazines—and never get horsewhipped. She knew that the same as everybody else in town knew it. But she had guts enough to live by it. And a dame with that kind of nerve will leave her gun home after two years. You can buy that or not. It made sense to me.

There was one more reason why I didn't figure Karen for Whipper's murder. If she had to split the money with Whipper, it meant a quarter million for her. If she killed him it meant half a million. A guy with five bucks might kill for ten and takes his chances with the chair. He's practically broke, he might even kill for less. But how many with a quarter of a million free of taxes would kill for that much again? Ask yourself if you would. I did, sitting there in the subway station. I got back "no" for an answer.

That's why I wondered about the way the cops had it figured. If Karen killed him, then she took it on the lam right after. But what if she wasn't even there when he called? Now that made sense. Kill for an extra quarter-million? No. But just run off with it. Why not?

The train came roaring into the station then like it was apologizing for keeping me there twenty minutes. I got up and walked to the doors. They hissed open. And with them an idea hissed through my head. Maybe Karen didn't kill Whipper or run out on him. Maybe Kincaid's boys got there first and persuaded her to leave with them. They had her address. They'd pummeled that much out of me. There was only a question of the time schedule.

I walked into the car and sat down. I started figuring the time. I left Kincaid's place around nine o'clock the night before. Hauptman and the others beat Karen's address out of me a minute or two later. I got to Maura's around nine-thirty and left there about ten-fifteen. That put me outside Karen's self-service elevator around ten-thirty—more than an hour after I'd turned over the address to Hauptman. Kincaid's boys had that much time to get over to the apartment and grab Karen with the cash. And maybe even shoot down Whipper if he happened to surprise them on the way out. A busy night, but easy enough for Kincaid's little darlings.

I figured the time schedule twice to see if I had it right. The numbers started going round and round in my head. The train wheels clacked through the empty car. I dozed off.

When I came to there were six million people squeezed and crushed every which way in the car. School kids, stenographers, truck drivers, salesmen, shopkeepers, office boys, the whole town. They were crammed together like so many strawberries in a jar of jam. And there I was slumped over two big, fat seats. I had slept through right up to the rush hour, eight-thirty by my watch. I must have ridden up and down the length of Manhattan three times.

What finally awakened me was one of the stenographers. She was yelling and flicking a pair of brown cotton gloves under my nose. "I pay my money the same as you. You get two seats and I got to stand down to Fourteenth Street. Who are you, the mayor's brother?" Then she swatted me over the head with the gloves.

What do you do? What do you say? What *can* you say? "Beg pardon." Then you kind of curl up against the wall and die until the next stop. Then you scram out the doors, up the stairs and grab a taxi.

In the taxi I began to wake up. First with my eyes, everything started looking bigger, clearer, brighter around me. Then with my ears, the sound of the taxi motor, the morning traffic, kids chasing each other to school with loud cowboy whoops. And finally with my nose and stomach. We hit one red light near a bakery, and the smell of warm bread ran through my nose and around my brain and down into my belly. When we got within a couple of blocks of my house I told the hacky to pull up. Then I paid him off and headed for my breakfast joint.

On the corner I stopped to pick up a copy of the paper. When I'd settled down with some orange juice, before the serious eating, I spread out the paper and gave it a quick eye. The Whipper case was the number one story. But it was just straight coverage. There was no mention of a tie-up between Sam Baniff's death and Whipper's. Tucked down near the bottom paragraph was a line about a "local newspaperman who arrived at the scene of the crime before the police and was asked to assist the investigation." They put it real pretty and they didn't even identify me. A nice job in all.

After that I opened the paper to my favorite column, "Boyd's Nest." The teasers for K. L. were all there. The bait was out and the trap was geared. I folded up the paper and ordered griddle cakes, sausages and a pot of coffee. I ate like a fiend.

I lingered over the third cup of coffee, smoked a cigarette and through the restaurant window I watched Greenwich Village going off to work. It was the late morning crowd, mostly white-collar workers, advertising copy writers, smalltime radio executives and similar low orders. I paid the check, tucked the paper under my arm and trudged on home.

There was a cute little blonde sitting in the lobby when I walked in. She had her legs crossed and the skirt of her gray dress crept up over her knee and popped out between the folds of her bright cloth coat. She pulled the skirt down an inch when she caught my glance.

I rang for the elevator, folded my hands behind my

back and walked in a small circle whistling a piece from some opera, probably Verdi or Puccini. I like the Italian stuff. I wanted the blonde to know that she wasn't being leered at by an uncultured slob.

When I'd walked half the circle to where I was facing her again, I saw that she'd turned her head out toward the front door where she could watch the radio and advertising boys swinging off to work. She wasn't interested in my leer. But the coat had fallen back another inch and the skirt was back up again. Her legs were long and shapely and her stockings just a shade darker than most women wear in daylight. Very nice.

I went back to walking my circle. I finished one trip and came up in front of the elevator with my back to the blonde. There was a small mirror over the elevator button. I straightened my tie in the mirror and examined two blue spots that Hauptman and his helpers had left on my face. Behind my reflection I could see the blonde sitting straight up in her chair. She wasn't glancing idly out the door now, she was staring right at my back. I smiled into the mirror. She snorted once and yanked her skirt back down.

The elevator door opened and Joe, the elevator operator, stepped out before I could enter. I gave him a good morning, but he motioned me aside with his head.

In the corner of the lobby he turned and leaned into me. "Mr. McGee," he whispered, "I thought I'd better let you know before—"

The blonde bounced off her chair and headed right for us. "Mr. McGee? You're Mr. McGee?"

I turned to her. "Just one minute, lady. My friend here has a message for me."

She stopped a foot away and turned her bright face up to mine. "Never mind that. He only wants to tell you that I've been pestering him for an hour now about when you'd be back." She smiled at Joe. "And now he's back and I won't be any more bother. You've been ever so sweet." Joe blushed and walked back to the elevator.

"You want to see me?" I asked the blonde.

"Urgently. I'm not one to make early morning calls without reason, Mr. McGee. This is a matter of life or death."

She said it like she was ordering a cream puff and tea. As she talked she pushed the fingers of her gloves up toward her hand one by one, straightening each seam. The scent of Oriental blossoms floated up from her. Not a cheap, heavy smell. Something around eight dollars an ounce.

"Whose life and whose death?" I asked.

"Yours," she said.

I looked her up and down once. Then I smiled and chucked her under the chin. She didn't shriek. She didn't giggle. And she didn't flap her arms and chirp like a bird. She wasn't out-and-out crazy. "You sure you've got the right McGee? There's two hundred and forty-nine in this year's phone book."

"Perfectly sure."

I shrugged and headed for the elevator, motioning for her to follow. She swung in behind me, her three-inch heels clicking across the stone floor and then getting lost as we reached the center carpeting. We stepped into the elevator and Joe took us upstairs.

I led the blonde down to my apartment and unlocked the door. After I'd switched on the lights and hung her coat away I motioned for her to make herself at home, and I walked back into my den. I tossed my coat and jacket on a chair, took off my tie and opened my collar. I was going to put on some slippers but I didn't know how the blonde would go in for that kind of informality. Instead I went into the bathroom, splashed some cold water on my face and let the faucet run on my wrists for half a minute.

By the time I'd finished up and gone back to the living room, she had made herself at home. But good. Her shoes were on the floor and she was sitting in the big blue chair with her feet tucked under her like the sexiest, gold-topped Buddha you ever saw. And here I'd hesitated about using a perfectly decent-looking pair of slippers.

"That lobby is terribly damp," she said, slipping one foot out from under her and rubbing it between her hands.

"Right." I sat down on the couch and pulled both my shoes off, chucking them near hers. "I'd brew up some coffee but I'm fresh out," I said.

"A whiskey would go better," she said.

I looked at her through one eye. "In the middle of the morning?" She gave her foot an extra hard rub. I got up and started back to the den in my socks. "It must have been a regular swamp in that lobby."

I poured us both good shots from the Haig and Haig bottle and told myself that it really wasn't early morning for me. I'd just finished a day's work. I always say that just before I take a morning shot. It makes me feel less like a candidate for Alcoholics Anonymous.

When I got back she was rubbing the other foot. She stopped long enough to take the glass from me and put the whiskey away with one belt. She didn't cough or shudder. But I got a side glance of her eyes tearing up like she'd just cut an onion. It must have cost her a lot to get that Scotch down.

Now I got the whole picture. The little blonde was playing a role. She was making like the smart, sophisticated lady in a comedy about high society. I smiled and sat back down on the couch, deliberately drinking my Scotch with slow, measured sips. She went back to rubbing her pretty feet with one hand.

"You want to tell me about this life and death matter now?" I asked. "Or should we wait for the butler to serve the canapes?"

She froze. Then her head turned up slowly and her eyes met mine. In a half-dream she reached down to the floor and put her glass there. "You think I'm pretty much of a fool, don't you?"

"To put it straight, I don't know what you are."

She nodded and tucked her foot back under her, brushing her skirt into place at the same time.

"Mr. McGee, my name is Helen Brooks. I am private secretary to Kingsley Benson. I'm here to save you from him."

I sat up and finished off the whiskey. No more games now. The horses were running again and the track was fast. "He sent you here to tell me that?"

"No, you've got it all wrong. He'd fire me in a second if he knew I was with you."

"What makes you think your boss is out to murder me, Helen?"

"I didn't say that. But he's angry enough to want to."

"So if he's not going to take a crack at me what's all this life-and-death talk?"

She leaned forward in the chair and the gray, tweedy material of her dress pulled tight across her breasts.

She wasn't a small woman. Just neat. "There are more ways than one to destroy a man. I imagine this morning's newspapers fit right in with Mr. Benson's plans. He's going to let the police pin the Whipper murder on you."

She reached for her handbag. It was a big, black thing with accordioned sides. She snapped it open and took out a folded copy of a morning paper. It wasn't my paper. She unfolded the paper and handed it to me. The headline read, "Columnist Quizzed in Gangland Slaying." There was an ugly picture of me, pulled out of some dusty file drawer and splashed over half the page.

I got it all from the first paragraph. They weren't sticking their necks out any to hang the thing on me, but it was pretty bad. I'm not the best loved newspaperman in town. All they could really hint at was that I tried to leave the scene of a crime without reporting it and that I arrived there mysteriously before the killing had been made known to the press. But the funny part of the story was that it made them look like they were browned-off because I'd gotten a newsbeat on them.

I dropped that paper next to the other one on the floor and sat back on the couch. "Not so bad," I said. "They're just hinting at things. The cops aren't pressing any charges and that's as far as it will go."

"And if the police don't find the murderer within the next day or two?"

"They might get anxious. They might haul me in again and talk things over. But what makes you think they won't get their man before then?"

"Because Kingsley Benson's their man and they'll never catch him."

"You just talking or have you got something behind you?"

She leaned forward again and the gray tweed pulled tight against her firm breasts. "I've got this. Kingsley Benson wasn't seeing this Lamain woman for entertainment. It was business. Benson hired her to help him fight a divorce action his wife is bringing."

"Come again?"

She put one hand to her throat. "Karen Lamain was paid to act as a—I believe you'd call it a decoy. She telegraphed Mrs. Benson in Reno, telling her that she, Karen, had evidence that would assure Mrs. Benson's divorce action. That's what Benson paid her for."

This was beginning to ring a bell. "Did the wife fall for it?"

"She did. She sued for a million dollars. She needed all the help she could get. Benson was betting on that when he hired the Lamain woman."

"So she came back East to meet with Karen?"

She nodded. "The plan, naturally, was for Miss Lamain to set up a rendezvous with Mrs. Benson and then have Benson and some witnesses barge in and discover his wife there. That would automatically destroy her residence requirement in the State of Nevada."

"That much I know. But how do you get from there to the Whipper killing?"

"What Kingsley Benson didn't realize was that he was dealing with a very shrewd young lady. Miss Lamain was paid five hundred dollars to lure Benson's wife into New York. So why not collect as much again for letting Mrs. Benson know, once she'd been tricked into coming here, just what her husband was plotting?"

"The double-cross," I said. This Lamain doll was more than pretty. She was a shrewd cookie.

"Precisely," the blonde said. "Now up to this point I'm certain of my facts. Since Mr. Benson trusts me implicitly he took me into his confidence during the initial planning. But once this double dealing took place Mr. Benson continued on his own."

"How'd you get wind of the switch then?"

"The original plan was for Benson to show up at the Lamain apartment at ten o'clock last night, at which time Mrs. Benson would have arrived as instructed. But yesterday afternoon a phone call came in for Mr. Benson, moving the appointment up to midnight. He was out of the office at the time and I relayed the message to him later that evening. He immediately suspected that Miss Lamain was conspiring to expose the scheme to his wife in return for money."

I laughed. "It wasn't for bubble gum, honey."

She nodded. "Mr. Benson was enraged. He decided to ignore the message and to proceed to the apartment at ten o'clock as planned. He hoped to catch his wife there before the Lamain woman could make her deal."

"Smart man. Did he follow through on that?"

"He did. He left for the Lamain apartment at nine-thirty."

"Left from where?"

Her face drained free of color. "Why—uh—uh—from the office."

"You work late, honey. Real late." I skipped over that for the minute. "So you figure he got up to the Lamain place about the time that Whipper was arriving, killed Whipper and retreated."

"Yes."

I smiled. "Fine. Only why kill Whipper? He had

nothing to do with the double-cross."

She ran her hands along her thighs and knees, smoothing the gray tweed skirt. "Revenge, I imagine. He came to the Lamain place to revenge that woman's treachery. When he got there he probably found Whipper. One word led to another and—" She shrugged.

I got up and fished a pack of cigarettes from my pocket. She didn't want one. I lit up and stood over her for a minute, staring at her large brown eyes, her honey-toned hair, the swell of breasts and thighs beneath the tweed dress. She was a pretty woman. It was too bad about that.

"I wish I could believe you ... Miss Brooks."

"Helen," she corrected. She didn't seem disturbed at being called a liar.

I nodded. "Helen, I wish I could believe you."

"What part don't you believe?"

"All of it."

She pulled her feet out from under her and jumped up in front of me. "But why?" She stood staring up at me from eight inches below. If she looked straight ahead she could see eye to eye with the second button on my shirt. She smelled good. She looked even better.

I turned and walked a few feet away. "First of all, the story—particularly that part about Benson killing Whipper out of revenge—that stinks. Secondly, there's the question of what you're doing here to begin with. Why all this concern over me, a guy you never saw in your life until now? Why rat on your own boss just to save my neck? What's your motive, honey?"

"I didn't want to see an innocent man framed," she said.

"Tch tch." I wiped an imaginary tear from my eye.

She clenched her firsts. "I didn't want you to die for a crime that Benson committed."

"Tch-tch-tch."

She raised her voice. "I didn't want it to be on my conscience."

"Tch-tch-tch-tch."

She ground her eyes shut. "I hate him," she screamed.

"Ahh," I said. "Now we're talking."

She threw her face into her hands and sobbed quietly. I led her back to the chair and sat her down.

"If you'd said that from the start it would have made sense."

She rubbed her eyes and sniffed once or twice before she smiled. "I thought if I told you about Benson and me you'd never believe the rest." She pulled the V-neck of her dress away from her body, reached inside and withdrew a small handkerchief. In that split second two lovely, round, full globes were half revealed, hidden only by the lower patchwork of a black strapless bra. She dabbed at her eyes with the handkerchief. She smiled again.

"You're looking at the prize chump of them all," she said. "I'm not only a private secretary to Kingsley Benson. I'm his butler when he needs a butler, his bartender when he needs a bartender and his wife when he needs one of those. All that for a hundred a week and a promise."

"Don't tell me," I said. "Let me guess. He swore he was in love with you. He told you his wife was a monster. And he swore that he would marry you the moment his wife would free him, right?"

"You named it. That was three years ago. And every week since we've been through it over and over again.

Each time it was the same: 'My wife won't let me go.' And I believed him."

"Then came the dawn," I said.

"Yes. His wife finally grew as fed up with him as he was with her. So she started a divorce suit. That should have made everything just fine. But it didn't."

"He gave you the brush?"

"Half a brush. The stick end," she said.

"He wouldn't keep the marriage promise he made. But he wanted to go right on playing kneesies with you." It was the oldest story in the world.

"It's a tough break for a girl," she said. "Three years shot to hell."

She was dealing from the top of the deck now, none of this "I want to save you … I want to protect the innocent … etc., etc." Now she was just a woman who'd been kicked over. And she was out to even the score. That was okay with me.

"Now it makes sense," I said. "Your heart wouldn't bleed much if I could prove that Benson killed Whipper, right?"

"It wouldn't bleed a drop."

I smiled. "Maybe you got a deal, lady. Only where do we go from here?"

"You know more about that than I. You're a newspaperman. But I imagine the next step is to get a look at Karen Lamain's apartment."

I laughed. "Scene of the crime stuff, eh? That only works in the movies. The cops have been crawling all over that place since last night. By now they've vacuumed the rugs, cleaned out the closets, dusted the walls for fingerprints and all the rest. The trail would be frozen stiff."

She thought about that for a minute. "We could try,"

she said finally. "We know what to look for. The police don't."

"We do?"

"Of course. Some sign that Benson was there last night."

"I thought we knew that already."

"Knowing it and proving it are two different things. I know Benson went there because he said so. But he'll deny every word of it. So there has to be proof. Once we have that we can go to the police, charge him with killing Whipper and—"

"—Save my carcass. It's a good deal. You pay back Benson for the three years you lost and I get my neck out of the noose at the same time."

She reached out and touched my cheek with the tips of her fingers. Her smile was warm and she was relaxed now. "Then you'll do it," she said.

"No, but I'll think about it. There's no rush. Since the cops cleaned the joint already, we'll find as much there next year as we will today."

"Whatever you say." Her fingers moved along the side of my face and around the back of my neck like four pink little marching men. "I feel better now. It's not just paying Benson back that's good. It's helping you. I came here out of petty spite, revenge, and all that talk about saving you was just a blind. But now it's different."

Her hand moved up and down the back of my neck, running the grain of the hair in and out between her fingers.

"How different?"

"Thirty minutes ago you were a name in a newspaper. Now you're a friend. A very nice friend."

She'd been leading up to this all along, only she

didn't know how to do it. She was self-conscious. She wasn't just trying to buy my support in convicting this Benson guy of murder. It was simpler than that. She was on the rebound. With some women if you lock them out of the house, they'll walk right into the next one just to prove they've still got a key that works. That's what she was proving, to herself more than to me or Benson.

"I don't mind being friendly now and then, Helen," I said. "But—" She slid her other arm around my neck and reached up at me with her lips. They were sweet, soft and warm against mine. Her tongue rolled out and twisted between my teeth. The phone rang. "Phone," I said.

"Let it ring," she said. She pulled my head down and we kissed again. The phone went on ringing. I pulled back.

"Maybe—" I said.

"No," she said. She turned my head to one side and ran her tongue along the cheek and around the rim of the ear. Her hand slid the length of my back down to my sit bone and then worked its way around. I pulled her in close and let my hand dip into the V-neck of her dress.

"No," she said. I picked her up and carried her into the bedroom. She never said another no. I guess the phone quit finally.

CHAPTER TWELVE

Later we dozed off. I had a dream. I dreamed that Maura walked into the room. She was dressed crazy, a big blue ribbon in her hair and a kid's skirt that came up over her knees. She was chewing gum and pulling it out of her mouth in a sticky string the way kids do. When she saw Helen and me lying in bed her hand stopped in mid-air and the gum dripped down like a suspension bridge. All she said was, "All right for you, Boyd McGee."

I woke up, stumbled into the bathroom and washed my mouth out with antiseptic. It was only when I walked back to bed that I realized Helen was gone. Her strange perfume still hung in the air and there was a note lying on her pillow.

Sweet: I'm still a working girl. Benson will probably tear his hair out when I walk in two hours late. But think what he'd do if he knew who I'd been with. Please take care of yourself. Love.

It was signed with red lip prints.

My watch said twelve-fifteen. I showered, shaved and dressed. That gave me twenty minutes of think time. I spent most of it on Helen Brooks. Her need to repay Benson for the kick in the teeth he gave her made sense. And her attempt to hide that motive at first was understandable enough. But there was something too pat about the whole situation, like she had staged it right down to the last love scene.

I finished the shower and shave and was pulling a shirt on when the phone rang again. I figured it was the party who'd been trying to get me earlier. I picked up the phone and gave whoever it was a cheery hello.

"McGee," he rasped. I recognized his growl right then.

"Hauptman," I said. "You're calling about my health,

I imagine, you scummy rat."

"Yeah, your health. Yours and somebody else's."

"I don't want to talk to you by phone, bub. The next time I speak to you it's going to be with a gun, an ax or a cleaver. Now blow!"

"Don't hang up, McGee. I've got a message from a friend —a lady friend. Miss Page says you should cooperate with us so's to keep her in good health."

I gripped the phone tighter and fought to keep the concern out of my voice. "You're not just a crook," I said "You're a lying crook. You're saying you've got Maura Page locked away some place. You're full of it!"

"Try me and find out," he said. "She's a redhead with curls on the forehead and cut close in back. She's got a kind of foreign kisser, all bone and thin eyes. Her lips—"

"That much you could have gotten from the papers or a copy of *Who's Who*," I said. But I didn't believe it.

"She's got a birthmark, too." He laughed. "That you don't read about in the papers."

I clenched my fist till I could feel the pain of nails dug into flesh. "What does he want?" I whispered.

"The same as yesterday," Hauptman said. "Karen Lamain's address."

"That's changed since yesterday."

"Yeah. He saw your column this morning. He figures if anybody finds her it'll be you. And maybe you've even heard from her this morning."

"No."

"Well, you will. And when you do you'll get right in touch with us, won't you? Maura says she wants you to. Oh, and just in case you think you can hold out on us, Kincaid says there's a time limit. You've got till midnight. After that, goodbye Maura. You get me?"

How could he figure I wouldn't get him? He was about as subtle as an air drill. "Look, Hauptman, what if I don't hear from the Lamain woman by then? What if—"

"Tough," he said. "That's the chance you take."

"The chance I— But what about her? She had nothing to do with—"

"She'll be fine until tonight. After that it's up to you, McGee. And personally I hope you make it. She's a pretty kid to be dying so young." The phone clicked.

I didn't hang up. I held the phone another minute until I was sure Hauptman was off the line. Then I spoke again.

"Cop." No answer. "You with the earphones." Still no answer. "Look, I know you're there. You've been there since they released me from the Centre Street jailhouse. Now let's not play games, officer. Speak up." I got another earful of silence. Then there was a click and a familiar humming sound. He'd just turned on a recording unit. "Okay, so you don't answer back. Just so long as you can hear me.... Some of Kincaid's boys must have tailed me to Maura Page's place last night. Now get these names straight because they'll mean something to Captain Fallon. Kincaid's crowd has grabbed Maura and they're using her to force information from me.

"I haven't got that information and I wouldn't make the deal if I had. So I'm going up to Kincaid's to try and release the Page woman. I'll need help later, maybe a half dozen or so cops. Only they've got to lay low until I make my play. If Kincaid's men smell cop they'll kill the girl. You got all that?" Still no answer. "Okay, see that you get it to Fallon on the double." I hung up.

I pulled on a tie and jacket and checked my coat to see if the gun was still there. A lot of good that had done me when Hauptman and his friends jumped me from behind. But it was better than nothing. And sooner or later my luck was in for a good turn.

I didn't bother with the elevator. I pounded down the three flights of stairs to the lobby and stopped only long enough to grab the morning mail from my box and shove it in my coat pocket.

I found a cab without any trouble and directed him to a spot two blocks from Kincaid's restaurant and office. Then I settled back and tried to figure my next move. That didn't get me much. The strategy would have to grow out of the situation.

I shuffled through the mail, separating bills and ads from personal letters. There were just three letters. One was from a St. Louis reporter I'd once worked with. He wanted to touch me for a hundred bucks. The second was from a fan in Ohio who'd gotten hold of my home address and written direct instead of to the office. He wanted advice on breaking into the newspaper racket. I get about twenty of those letters a week at the office.

The third one wasn't a letter at all. There was no return address on the envelope. I slit it open and out popped this coil of steel wire. I picked up one end, let it unroll a foot or so and then I could see what it was. A foot of wire and then a knot and then a loop. Someone had fashioned a miniature noose and mailed it to me. It was a simple enough message. Kincaid was putting the screws on me from all sides. He wanted the half million and he was willing to spill blood for it—lots of blood and all mine.

I slipped the noose back into the envelope and shoved

it into my pocket. Then I lit a cigarette and settled back, watching the streets fly past. I thought about Sam Baniff's funeral. Sam's only living kin was a brother in Bensonhurst. He'd be the one making the funeral arrangements. I wanted to send some flowers.

Thinking about Sam's funeral brought me back to Maura Page. She did a favor for a newspaperman she'd known for one night, she patched his battered body and fed him some broth. For that the boys who killed Sam were planning the same for her. Whether they did it or not was up to me. If I found a way the girl would live. If not ... So I sat in the cab riding up to Kincaid's place and I puffed on a cigarette and I felt like an old man.

There was something else facing Maura Page. Something close to death. Insanity. That was no solid, balanced brain she carried with her. The wires in her head were drawn as tight as piano strings, ready to pop under any strain. I don't know how the psychoanalysts would have defined her state but I figured her to be about two screams this side of the nut house. What she needed was kindness and attention. What she'd get from Kincaid's boys didn't fit that bill.

I just prayed I could get there before the strings began popping. I'd seen a good mind go that way once and that was enough. There was this kid I knew who wrote himself a hell of a good play and got a Hollywood contract. His old man had made three million bucks in the toilet seat business. But when the kid said he wanted to write plays, poppa cut him off without a penny. The kid starved in a cellar for three years before his first play made the grade and a studio signed him up. So he jumped into Hollywood with both feet. Big house, big swimming pool, big car, big women, big opium, big everything. They brought him back to New York in a straitjacket. His poppa wanted him near where he could visit him regularly.

And thinking about the playwright who blew his cork, I began to understand a little more about Maura. She liked boys. Not just one or two, here and there. Not just tall ones with blond curls or lean ones with shell-rimmed glasses. Any kind, tall or short, lean or fat, with or without glasses. She liked boys.

I hadn't bothered wondering what made her that way. But thinking about the nutty boy-author whose old man was the toilet seat king, I began picturing Maura's childhood. A mother up to her jade earrings in Newport, Palm Beach and Riviera society, a father up to his pinky diamond ring in stock quotations and floating loans. And an older sister, the last refuge of a lonely girl, with a head full of expensive gowns and air. Drop a sensitive girl with a dream to paint some pictures into the middle of that mess and you're going to get a sour note somewhere.

I pulled down the cab window, flipped the cigarette out into the street and gulped some air. A bleak sky covered the city. The cab was at Madison Avenue and Fifty-ninth Street. Kincaid's was half a dozen blocks off. I took the gun from my pocket, threw the safety catch off and returned it to my inside pocket. That's a bad practice, walking around with an automatic off safety. You can trip and shoot a hole in your belly. But if you're planning to draw against five other men then you'll take your chances on tripping for the extra second you gain with the safety off.

CHAPTER THIRTEEN

The cab pulled to the curb in another minute, and I hopped out and paid the hackie off. I began walking the two blocks to Kincaid's place. When I'd reached the end of the first, just a block east of Kincaid's, I could see a man standing diagonally across the street, coat collar up and hat brim down all around. I recognized his slump. It was one of the men who'd beaten my head in the night before.

I hotfooted it completely around the block, coming up on the west side of the street. There was a man working that corner too. I never saw him before but I didn't have to. He was cut from the same cheap metal they use to make all gunmen. I didn't bother looking any further. I figured there must have been four or five men covering the place. I'd never stand a chance with a direct approach. But I knew one thing now for sure, Maura Page was in that building somewhere.

I scooted back down the street and around the corner. The building ran clear through the block and there was nobody covering the back end. But that didn't do much good since the only door back there was a service entrance into the restaurant kitchen. Even if I could get through there past the kitchen help and up to the first floor, I'd still have to run three floors of muscles and guns. What I needed was a helicopter.

I walked along the rear of Kincaid's building till it came to an end in the middle of the block and another began. The two buildings were much alike. I stepped across the street for a long view. The buildings were identical. The whole block had probably been owned by one real estate outfit at some time and they built the twin buildings. From the front it was hard to tell this, since Kincaid had prettied his up with a large canopy, some potted plants and a lot of black and gold trimming. But from the rear the buildings were identical.

A narrow alley separated the two. But when I say narrow I mean narrow. Maybe there was three feet of clearance in all. Whatever the minimum separation demanded by the Health Department, that's all the landlord put in. The sun probably hit each wall for a total of three and a quarter minutes a day. That wasn't important, though, since the architect who planned the buildings had left those walls blank except for two rows of facing windows. They were long, narrow, frosted windows—bathroom windows.

A quick image of Kincaid's third-floor office popped into my head. One entrance was from the reception room where the loan society members gathered. The other was from a black-and-white tiled bathroom which probably led in turn to the rest of his personal suite. I looked up at the narrow frosted window on the third floor of Kincaid's building. Unless there was more than one bathroom per floor that window would lead me straight to Kincaid.

The building that faced Kincaid's also had a service entrance at the rear. I walked in the door and down a steep ramp that led past garbage cans and stacks of old newspaper to an elevator. It was a self-service car. That was a good break. I pushed the button and waited, using the time to sketch a mental diagram of the house so I would know just which apartment faced Kincaid's. The side of Kincaid's building faced east. I was looking for a third-floor apartment with a bathroom window that faced west.

I found it but it wasn't easy. There were only two apartments per floor, which should have made it a cinch. So I picked the one that should have fit the description and rang the doorbell. A short, skinny gray-haired old man in pants and undershirt opened the door a crack and looked me up and down.

"She ain't here," he said, and slammed the door.

I rang again, leaning on the bell for all it was worth. He opened the door wide this time. "Now look, son, I told you once she ain't here. So—"

"I didn't come to see her, Pop."

He laughed. "Maybe you come calling on me, eh?" From his back pocket he took a pair of wire spectacles. He must have broken a pair every time he sat down. He slipped them on and pushed his face toward mine. "Say, I ain't never seen you around here before. You must be one of the new ones."

"I'm trying to explain it to you, Pop, I don't know your daughter."

"Course not. It's my granddaughter you know. My daughter is still out in Arizona. You're lucky you don't know her, son. She's the battle-axe of Skull County."

I let my jaw drop like it had suddenly become too big a load to tote. "Skull County?" I gasped. "Not *the* Skull County! Not Skull County, Arizona!"

His eyes lit up like twin birthday candles. "You know it? You been there?" His hands shook and his face nodded expectantly. This was the big thing in the old man's life, for sure.

"Know it?" I said. "Does a coyote know its young? Does a cactus have needles? Does a rattlesnake bite?"

He laughed a reedy, crackling laugh. "You know it! You know it! It's God's country and you know it." He opened the door another inch or two.

"Know it?" I repeated. "Is the high noon hot as Hades? Is the night as cold as deep freeze? Are the rivers dried-up mud holes?"

He cackled. "Yes, you know it and it's paradise." The door swung open another two or three inches and I made a dive for it. I got halfway through before he knew what was happening. I blurted out the story as I went.

"I'm nuts about Arizona, Pop. I may even go there some day. But look, there's a girl being held against her will in an apartment across the alley from here. The only way to her is through a bathroom window that faces west. There are only two apartments on this floor, so it's two to one that yours is the one."

"The one what?" He was confused. And he was disappointed that all that scrumptious talk about Arizona had come to an end.

"The one with the bathroom that faces west."

He nodded once or twice and then his face turned sour before my eyes. "Bet you ain't never been west of Philadelphia, smart guy. And you want to see some wet rivers, you just come to Arizona in the rainy season, smart guy. And further, it ain't none of your business which way my bathroom faces." He started to slam the door again but I was past that stage.

"Look, Pop, I'm bigger than you. I can force my way in if I want. But I might need your help. There's a rat that walks on two feet by the name of Kincaid and—"

The door flew open and I nearly fell on my head diving in. He gave me that cackling laugh again. "Well, for sweet frying oysters, whyn't you say you was hunting for this Kincaid to begin with? Any enemy of that skunk is a friend of mine." He stuck out his hand

and I gave it a quick shake. "Craggs is my name. Hendley Craggs. You can call me Hank."

"Thanks," I said. "Now about that—"

"Yes sir, if there's any way I can help to hogtie this Kincaid why you just tell me how. Because that man is about the lowest order of living thing there is. Now just let me show you something." He grabbed me by the arm and pulled me down the corridor past a huge, richly furnished living room. There was a large, framed picture of a pretty girl standing on a mahogany table. The girl was naked from head to toe except for two long scarves held in either hand and used to cover the more critical areas.

The old man caught me admiring the picture and stopped pulling me down the hall. "A real doozey, ain't she? Of course Billie—that's my granddaughter—she don't like to keep it up there in the living room."

"That's understandable," I said. "A man your age, pop. I mean—"

"Son, she's my granddaughter and I'd be proud of her no matter what."

"Your— You mean the dame in the picture and your granddaughter are—"

"—one and the same. Yes sir, Billie is one of the top attractions at the Jersey City Burlesque, across the river. They don't permit no burlesque here in New York, you know."

I smiled. "I get it now, Pop. You figured me for one of the stage-door johnnies trailing your granddaughter."

"Wouldn't be a bit surprised if you still turned out to be one. You boys use an awful lot of tricky ways to get past a door. But I'm twice as foxy as most of you. That's how I'm back here in this rotten, rheumatic city instead of out in the Arizona sunshine. You didn't think we'd let Billie come East without an escort, did you?"

"To tell the truth, Pop—"

His face turned a light purple hue. "Well, we wouldn't, see? Some of you boys get funny notions. You think just because a girl wiggles around a dance floor practically naked to make a living that it means—"

"No I don't, Pop. I don't think that at all."

His face went from light to dark purple. "Well, you'd just better not, son, if you know what's good for you. 'Cause the first man I catch—" The veins bounced out of his forehead and he ran out of breath.

"Easy, Pop. I'm not here about your granddaughter, remember? I came about this man Kincaid."

He coughed once or twice and sucked in air through his mouth until he could regain his breath. "Kincaid, eh? Well, just let me show you what that snake of a man and his gang did to—"

He started leading me down the hall again. "No, look, Pop, all I want to know is whether your bathroom faces—"

"Well, what do you think I'm showing you?" We came face to face with a door and the old man pushed it open. It was a bathroom door. He walked in and motioned me to follow while he pushed up the window. A cold blast of air billowed the rose shower curtain. "I'm a self-dependent man, son. I once lived five years on the desert without another single soul. I'm used to doing my own cooking, cleaning and washing. Now just let me show you what that snake Kincaid did to me."

He leaned out the window and grappled with something out there for a minute. "Ahhh, here it is."

He stepped back from the open window and came away with a piece of rope in his hand. It was about four feet long with one end tied to a metal hook set in the window frame. The other end was frayed a bit.

"You see, I just made myself a simple lasso, tied one end to the window here and twirled it across the alley to where it hooked onto the other window. It was the neatest little clothes line you ever saw. Nothing big, mind you, held maybe two pairs of socks, one pair of long johns and a handkerchief or two. So what does that Kincaid go ahead and do but cut it right, straight down. Yes sir, it's little things like that that tell a man's character. And I'll say it here and now, that Kincaid is a killer."

I walked to the window and stared out across the way. There was no more than a three-foot space between the windows. I leaned my body as far out as I could and reached out with one arm. The tips of my fingers touched the fronted window pane across the way. The window was closed tight. There was a way—one that would have been easy fifteen years earlier when I'd done it four-a-day in a vaudeville aerial act. But I was fifteen years older and slower and—and something had to be done.

I pulled my arm back in and shut the window on the cooling breeze that blew through the alley. "You got a crowbar or a good, strong screwdriver, Pop?"

He closed one eye in thought and then bounded out of the room. He was back in half a minute with a couple of six-inch nails. "You're gonna try to pry open that window, right? Well, one of these will do it, if she ain't locked. If she is it's too bad, 'cause I haven't got a crowbar in the house."

I took one of the nails and ran it around in my

fingers. He was right. Any window lock worth its price would bend that nail over backwards. But it was worth a try on the chance that Kincaid's window was open.

I chucked my overcoat off and laid it on the edge of the bathtub. I put my jacket on top of that and transferred the gun from the jacket to my pants pocket. The old man grinned at the weapon.

"I see you figured this Kincaid the same as me," he said. "He cut down your clothes line too?"

"Worse than that, Pop. He cut down a friend of mine."

The old man stopped grinning and rubbed his nose with the back of one hand. "I knew it. I knew it right off. A snake if I ever saw one. All right, mister, what's our next move?"

"I'm going through there, Pop." I pointed to the window. "If I can get through, that is. Then I'll need your help."

"I'm not packing a gun, son. Billie wouldn't let me bring it East when we come."

A smile started to break through the corners of my mouth and I fought it back. "That's all right, Pop. But there's something else you can do. You can hold on to my feet when I go out that window."

"Done." He stuck out his hand and I shook it. "You're as safe as a babe in bed, son. I used to be tug-a-war champion of Skull County." I opened the window, stuck one of the six-inch nails between my teeth and started to climb out. "Of course, that was back in nineteen ought seven or ought eight." I wished he hadn't added that.

I could reach the other ledge with my fingertips without leaving the floor but after that I had to start climbing. The old man held both my feet. I squirmed out the window up to my chest. By then I could practically lean my elbows on the other ledge. I pushed out as far as my belt and then I could rest my elbow on the ledge. I put the palm of my other hand flat against the window and pushed up. It wouldn't budge.

That didn't mean the window was locked but it wasn't a happy omen. I took the nail from my mouth and stuck it in the crack between window and casement. I pushed down. The nail slipped out. I tried it again. The nail slipped out again. Sweat was beginning to run down both sides of my face, cold April sweat.

The third time I tried the nail caught against something. I felt the window give a little on one side before the nail slipped out again. I moved the nail over to the other end and worked that for a while. It caught after half a dozen tries and the window budged again. So I kept at it, first one side, then the other, over and over and over.

It took maybe twenty minutes before I'd gotten it raised far enough to get my hand in under it. By then my forehead was covered with sweat, my left elbow was sore as a boil from being leaned on all that time and my fingers were ready to drop off. I flipped the nail aside, put one hand in the narrow opening under the window and pushed up. The window gave slowly, silently.

I turned back to the old man and held up one hand in the circle-and-three-finger salute. He let go a noisy cackle and I put a finger to my lips to hush him. Then I got both arms through the open window and indicated to the old man to let go of my feet. I pushed my head through the window, rested my chest on the ledge and then shoved down with everything I had.

My feet tumbled from the other ledge and swung

across the alleyway in a short arc. The upper half of me shot upward past the window ledge and into Kincaid's bathroom. For one moment there was this straight line from head to toes, half in the room, half out in the alleyway forty feet off the ground. Then I fell forward and tumbled into the room. From across the void of fifteen years I heard the roar of an audience, shouting, whistling, stamping their applause. It was the best performance I'd ever given. Now all I had to do was think up a good closer for the act.

I hit the tile floor with a loud thud and just lay there for a minute or two, listening for footsteps. There were none. I got up and closed the window. Then I spent a few minutes rubbing some circulation back into my fingers.

There were two doors in the room. One led to Kincaid's office, that much I knew. I figured that the other led back into his personal apartment. But I didn't know which was which. I put an ear to one. There were voices. In a minute's time I could make out four separate tones, but I couldn't tell a word any of them were saying. Suddenly one voice became louder and clearer. Someone was approaching the door.

I turned quickly to the other door. It was locked but there was a key on the bathroom side like you get in hotel rooms with connecting baths. I turned the key quickly, opened the door and stepped through.

The room I stepped into was pitch black. I closed the door behind me. A split second later I heard the other bathroom door open and someone enter. I slipped out my automatic and felt my way in the darkness till I reached the wall. I flattened myself against it and waited.

I heard whoever it was turn the water on and splash around for a minute. I pictured an ugly ape of a gunman carefully combing his shiny black hair and admiring his green teeth in the mirror. I waited for him to try the other door. He turned off the faucet and began fumbling around with the doorknob. I braced myself. He fumbled some more. His hands were wet. Finally he kicked it once, walked back out and closed the other door behind him.

I hunted around in the dark, trying to get a picture of the room with my fingers that I could transfer to my brain. I found a chair, a picture on the wall, a light switch, another chair and a bed. It was Kincaid's boudoir. The bedcover was a thick, satiny cloth with some kind of heavy embroidery. And in the middle of it was a naked body. The flesh was warm. I felt a hand, an arm, a shoulder, a breast. I swung around, made it back to the light switch and flipped it on.

Maura Page was lying in the middle of the bed, her eyes tightly closed. One wrist was bound with a rope. The other was free and in that hand she held a heavy cone of wood that rose to a vicious point. "One more step," she moaned. "Just one more and I'll brain you."

"Maura. Open your eyes. It's me, babe."

She didn't open them. Instead she began thrashing around on the bed, moaning and sobbing. She thought it was a dream. "Look at me, Maura. It's Boyd. I'm here. It's no dream."

The thrashing stopped. She opened one eye and gasped. She sat up quickly and grabbed my wrist. She closed her eyes and then opened them again. "It is," she said. "It is."

I sat down on the bed. "Is there another door out of here?" I whispered. She ran her hand up my arm to the shoulder and then back again.

"It is," she said. "It is."

"It's me, all right. And you're going to be just fine in a minute or so, if I can get us out of here. Now tell me, is there another door?"

"It is," she said.

I got a good look at her eyes then. They weren't clouded over. They were clear as crystal. But they didn't see anything. They stared out at me, never moving from my face, never changing expression. She was there beside me but she might just as well have been a thousand miles away.

I got up and cased the place. The bed was a big one, outsized. It was one of those four-poster affairs, colonial style. Each post was topped with a large brown shape made to resemble a pine cone. Kincaid's men had bound Maura on the bed and stripped her to prevent escape. But she had managed to slip the bonds and unscrew the huge pine cone from one of the bedposts. It made as good a weapon as any.

There was a wall of drapery at one end of the room. I pulled that away and found a big window that looked out. I could see the two gunmen at each end of the street. I pulled the drapes back into place.

There was no other door than the one that led to the bathroom and from there into Kincaid's office. Going back to the door, I opened it and removed the key. Then I went into the bathroom and inserted the key into the lock of the facing door, the one that led to Kincaid's office. I turned the key very quietly in the lock and then removed it. There might have been more than one key so I wadded up a matchbook cover and shoved it into the lock. The idea was to get Maura and me back out through the window before Kincaid knew anything.

There was a loud, thumping noise from the bedroom. I rushed back in and found Maura lying on the floor. Her feet were bound. I hadn't noticed that before. She'd tried to get off the bed and had fallen. I rushed to her and began untying the rope. She let go a piercing scream and began beating at me with the wooden cone. I twisted it out of her hand but she kept on screaming. I clipped her one on the chin and she passed out.

The joint was jumping now. The boys were pounding on the bathroom door. I rushed in there and threw open the window. Pop was still at the other window waiting for me.

"Cops!" I shouted, "Get around to your other window, Pop. Call out into the street. They're within a block of here, somewhere. Use a whistle or just shout your brains out. Only keep your head down. Kincaid's got the street covered with gunmen."

The old man laughed. "Whistle, hell. I got this." He held up a battered-looking bugle. "I blew this with Pershing in Mexico." He put it to his lips and gave a blast. Kincaid's men were battering the door with their shoulders now.

"Great," I yelled. "Only get around to the other side of the house where they can hear you. And keep your head down."

"Don't worry about me, son. It'll take more than them to stop an Arizona man." He gave another blast on the bugle and tottered off.

Kincaid was shouting from the other side of the door. "That's sheet metal, you fools. You'll never batter it down. Stand back."

I wondered when they'd get around to it. I raced out

the other door and locked it. There was a loud report. Kincaid had blown the first lock off.

I picked up Maura's limp body and carried it behind an upholstered chair. Then I took my place alongside the door, flattened against the wall. From the distance I heard the tortured wail of a bugle. But it sounded like sweet music to me.

"McGee!" It was Kincaid himself on the other side of the door. "I want to talk business. Let's leave the cops out of this."

"You should have thought of that before," I shouted. "Before you killed Sam. The cops are in it now, for good." There was another distant bugle blast.

"Then we'll deal them out. We'll give them a patsy."

"Keep talking."

"Open the door."

"Do it yourself, you're good at that." I switched off the lights and slipped across the room to where there was a tall walnut wardrobe. I plastered myself against that. There was another shot and the door flew open.

CHAPTER FOURTEEN

Kincaid stood there, a smoking gun in his hand. His eyes tried to cut through the darkened room. "McGee?" He made a perfect silhouette in the doorway. I raised my gun. "McGee? Look, I want to talk. See, I'm chucking my gun." He dropped the gun to the floor.

"Okay," I said. "Let's talk." That's all he wanted to know, my position in the room. His other hand came up. There was a flash of light and a roar. He'd been holding two guns. Kincaid only played sure things.

The bullet tore into the wall behind me. "So we don't

talk," I shouted. I held my fire. Time was with me, not him. He stepped out of the doorway and into the darkened room.

"Can't blame a man for trying," he laughed. "Okay, here's my proposition. You were right about Hauptman. He gunned your pal. I sent him out to throw a scare into Baniff. But Hauptman is gun-happy. I know that now."

"That must have come as quite a surprise," I said.

"Look, let's cut this deal fast, McGee. You know what I want. The cash. You can lead me to it. In return you get Hauptman and a big piece of change. That part still goes."

Another silhouette appeared in the doorway. Kincaid couldn't see him, his back was to the door. "Make it clear about Hauptman," I said.

"Like I said, you get him. What you do with him is your business. Turn him over to the cops or take care of him yourself. I figured that last part might appeal to you, seeing as this Baniff was such a good pal of yours."

The silhouette in the doorway raised one hand to waist level. I couldn't see it clearly but there was a gun there. There had to be. "So," I said, "Hauptman takes the rap for Baniff's murder and you and I grab the half million. Right?"

"Right."

"Okay," I said. "It's a deal. Hauptman takes the rap."

"You double-crossing—" That's all you could hear above the roar of a gun. Flame spurted from the silhouetted figure in the doorway.

I fired once. The figure remained standing for one second and then crumpled slowly to the floor.

There was a moment of total silence, broken only by

another far-off blast of a bugle. I knew I'd gotten my man. What I didn't know was whether he'd gotten Kincaid first. I held my position behind the wardrobe and waited. The lights came on.

Kincaid was standing over Hauptman's body. Kincaid was hit too. He held his right arm with his left hand and blood seeped through. But Hauptman was beyond that. My bullet had found its mark just below the heart. Blood flowed from his mouth and nose. One lung must have been punctured. Kincaid stared down at the body and a slow smile worked its way across his face. "You're a hero, McGee. You just shot a killer. And you just did yourself a big favor."

I stepped out from behind my cover. "How's that?"

Kincaid touched Hauptman's body with the tip of his shoe. Hauptman made a gurgling moan. "He killed Baniff, all right. But he didn't kill Whipper. The boys squeezed Karen Lamain's address out of you. When I heard the Whip had broken out of stir I sent Hauptman up to her place to grab him. Whipper knew where the money was and that's what I wanted. Hauptman never would have killed the man who could lead me to five hundred grand. But that's something only you and I know."

"So?"

Kincaid winced and bit down on his lower lip. The arm must have been giving him lots of pain. "So now Hauptman's at the end of his line and Baniff's murder is accounted for. So why not let Hauptman account for Whipper's murder too? According to the papers, the cops think you might have been mixed up in that. So now we got this body down here and we let it take the rap for both jobs. Hauptman won't mind." He nudged the body again and Hauptman gave another gurgling moan.

"You could fix that, could you?"

"You mean dummy up a motive? Sure. All we do is switch it around a little. The cops know somebody was behind Whipper's blackmail setup and they know Whipper double-crossed him. So now we let it drop that Hauptman here was the brains of the outfit." Kincaid laughed and then winced in pain again. "So Hauptman killed Whipper to revenge the double-cross."

"And what's in it for you?"

"The same as before. Karen Lamain is bound to contact you within the next twenty-four hours. You fox her into a rendezvous some place. Leave the rest to me. We'll get the money out of her."

"Suppose she won't talk?"

Kincaid bit down hard on his lip again and a thin trickle of blood rolled out of his mouth. "There are ways," he said. "It's not in my line but there are lots of boys who specialize in treating lockjaw. Especially with women. The ladies are very fond of their good looks. They'll do a lot to preserve a straight nose or an unmarred complexion, eh?"

"You could probably do it at that," I said. "But there's just one thing wrong with the setup, Kincaid. Hauptman is still alive. If he doesn't die—and soon—the whole thing isn't worth a damn."

Kincaid nodded. He dug his fingers deep into the wounded arm and the flow of blood slowed for a moment. "Yeah," he said. "There's that. But that shouldn't be hard to fix." He drew back one foot and kicked down at the body once, hard, right to the back of the head. "Hauptman was a hard man to stop. Even after you shot him you had to beat him to the ground with your own bare hands. Makes you an even bigger hero."

I bent over the body and felt one wrist. There was no pulse beat. The man who killed Sam Baniff was dead. That wouldn't do Sam much good but it made me feel a lot better.

I straightened up. There was a loud and confused babble of voices from the front of the apartment. I recognized Captain Fallon's bark. Kincaid's office was being invaded and his front guard was crumbling under the attack.

"Is it a deal?" he asked.

"A deal?" I picked the satin cover off the bed and went behind the upholstered chair where Maura lay in semi-coma. I wrapped the spread around her naked body and picked her up. "Sure it's a deal. All you've got to do is give this kid back her health. Then bring Sam Baniff back to life. And finally, put a bullet through your brain. Then you've got a deal."

Fallon came puffing through the bathroom door, driving three of Kincaid's men before him. Harry, the bespectacled croupier who wrote a book on investments, was one of the three. He licked nervously at his lips and ran a hand over the few wisps of hair that covered his scalp. He looked out of place between the two young gunmen.

"I'm an investment adviser by profession," he was saying. "I know nothing about this, sir."

"Shaddap!" Fallon roared. The red-headed lieutenant was there too, followed by half a dozen uniformed cops and old Pop, carrying the bugle in one hand and my jacket and overcoat in the other.

"Here's your man, Fallon." I nodded at Hauptman's body. "He killed Sam Baniff. I put a bullet through him in self-defense, but he was alive until a minute ago. Kincaid there finished him off. You'll probably find some blood and hair on Kincaid's shoe that'll prove it."

Pop came forward and threw my jacket and overcoat over my shoulders. "Good go, son. You're my kind of animal. If you ever need any more help of this kind give me a signal. This here town is quiet as a tomb, mostly."

"We'll want a deposition from you, McGee," the lieutenant said.

"Yeah, yeah, you'll get it. Only right now I've got to get his girl to a doctor." I started out of the room.

"Hey," Fallon yelled. "What about the Whipper killing and the money? What about that?"

"One damn thing at a time, Captain. You guys have to do *something* to earn your keep."

Pop followed me out to the hall and down the elevator. I hailed a taxi and Pop stood in the doorway and waved at me. I lowered Maura's silent body into the taxi seat and pulled the cover tightly about her. "Don't forget what I said, son," Pop called out. "Any time you need me just call out. This town is quiet as a tomb, mostly."

"Mostly," I said, and the taxi roared off.

The doctor I took her to was a nerve specialist by the name of Ervin, an Englishman who had quite a reputation in New York medical circles. I thought of contacting her folks to see if they wanted to use her family physician. But I knew she wouldn't want that and she was of legal age. Besides, I didn't go for the idea of explaining how I came to carry their daughter naked and in a state of coma out of the apartment of a prize citizen like Pete Kincaid.

The doctor didn't turn a hair when I carried her into the office and put her on his couch. He asked two simple questions. One, was she a diabetic? I said no. I'd seen her put away a pint of whiskey that first night at Club 41. No diabetic would try that, not even a crazy one.

Then he asked if she was a cardiac, I couldn't answer that. I didn't know anything about her heart except that it was in the right place. Especially when it came to helping out a newspaperman in distress.

Doctor Ervin went over her with a stethoscope. When he was reasonably convinced that her heart was in good shape, he examined her arms and then pulled down her eyelids. He was looking for signs of dope addiction. There were none.

He made a quick brain check with one of those encephalograph machines. That was probably to rule out epilepsy. After that he decided it was some form of shock and he had his nurse prepare a needle. That's when he made me leave the room.

I paced up and down the reception room waiting for word. It didn't come for half an hour. That gave me time to sweat and worry and to wonder why I cared so much about the pretty girl lying on the doctor's couch. After a while I began to understand it. It was like I had become the father she never really had. There was something so pitiable about the way she worked at being a wicked, dangerous female. She had the body of a woman, the brain of a woman, but the soul of a child.

The doctor came out smiling. She was out of it now. He explained that she needed immediate rest and later a thorough examination. He agreed to let her relax in his office until she was able to ride home. I paid him off and agreed to bring her around in a few days for a full examination.

I felt like a new man after that. I went out and ordered a five-course lunch. Then I picked up my car in front of Maura's place and drove down to the office. I got there around three o'clock.

They gave me one of those Lindbergh receptions. A couple of the girls had cut up some old newspapers into confetti and tape. I walked in the door and they threw this stuff at me. Hail the conquering hero. Also a good excuse to pass the bottle around and get looped in the middle of a work day.

My editor wasn't as happy. He gave me two quick pats on the back for having dropped Sam's murderer. Then he lammed it into me for not having reported in directly after the shooting. I tried to explain to him about Maura Page and the coma. That didn't cut any ice with him. I think what he was really sore about was that I worked for a morning paper but I'd been disloyal enough to shoot Hauptman in time for the evening editions.

I put in an hour at the office going over the mail and phone messages. There was a message from Lieutenant Governor Colombo. He was still in town and he was waiting for me to get some word from Karen Lamain. But there was no message from her.

The office mail brought me some live tips for the column. A few could be used right off but most of them had to be rechecked. From my pockets I pulled the morning mail that had come to my apartment and sorted it out. Most of it was strictly for File Number Thirteen—the waste paper basket. But there was that wire noose from Kincaid. That was worth saving. A memento of a prince among men.

Around four o'clock I drove down to Centre Street and gave Captain Fallon my deposition on the Hauptman shooting. The cops were friendlier than a fraternal order on a Sunday picnic. After all, hadn't I bagged Sam's killer just as I'd promised to? And wasn't I the only link to Karen Lamain, to say nothing of a half million dollars and the governor's spotless reputation? I'm telling you, that was McGee day all over town.

I decided to take advantage of the situation. I asked Fallon if he'd let me check through the stuff they'd taken from the Lamain apartment. He agreed to that. I think he'd have given me his toothbrush if I'd asked him nicely.

They dragged out the stuff: microphones, amplifiers, recording equipment, cameras, packets of letters and photographs—everything. I went over it for ten or fifteen minutes, particularly the letters from Whipper to his wife. There was nothing new in those except that I noticed the letters had been addressed to a New York post office box instead of directly to her apartment.

Everything had been done to hide Karen's whereabouts. And all of it had been undone by an accidental line in a Broadway column.

There was nothing for me there. What I wanted was possible proof that Kingsley Benson had been in Karen's apartment that night. Maybe just a cigar band or a match cover was all it would take. But the cops weren't looking for Benson so they might have walked right past that kind of proof. Helen Brooks was right; the only way to get that kind of evidence against her boss was to comb Karen's apartment first hand.

I left police headquarters and drove up to the Lamain apartment. I expected that it might have been sealed up by the cops, but it wasn't. They generally seal up the murder room until things get straightened out. But of course Whipper hadn't actually been killed in her apartment. He'd gotten it in the elevator. And you can't go around sealing up elevators unless you want every landlord in town down on your head.

I had a surprise waiting for me inside the apartment. The door was unlocked and somebody was prowling around the bedroom. I took out my automatic. It still smelled from cordite. I slipped off the safety and walked in on the prowler.

Prettiest prowler I ever saw. It was Helen Brooks, all five feet three of her, blonde and blushing. She got over that fast enough. She sighed with relief.

"I mean you nearly scared me to death, Boyd."

"That makes two of us." I slipped the safety back on and put the gun away. She came over and gave me a friendly pat on the cheek with her gloved hand.

"You'll never guess who sent me here," she said. I took her hand from my cheek and gave it a gentle squeeze. "Benson himself. How's that for luck? Here I'd been dying to get up and have a look around this place and then Benson orders me to do it."

"How come?"

"For the same reason I wanted to have a look. He thinks he might have dropped something here. A money clip with his initials on it."

I whistled. "He told you that today? He actually admitted being here last night?"

"Yes, but it's not all that you think it is. He swears that Whipper wasn't here then and that all he did was give the Lamain woman some extra cash to go through with the frame-up of Mrs. Benson. That's when he thinks he dropped the money clip."

"And you haven't been able to find it?" She shook her head. "Well, Benson's in the clear then. I just went over the things that the cops took from here. There wasn't a money clip among them."

She shook her head. "I don't think I'd tell him that. I think it's better if he goes on wondering whether or not the police found the clip and if they're building a case against him. I think Kingsley might break under that kind of strain. He's no superman."

I thought that was a fair idea. But I got an even better one. "Look, chicken, I think we can put the screws to this middle-aged Romeo lots faster with a little brainwork." She smiled, sat down on one corner of Karen Lamain's dressing table and crossed her neat, nyloned legs. "Suppose I pay your boss a visit and tell him that the money clip has been found—I found it. The cops don't know a thing about it yet. You see the play?"

She ran her teeth over her lower lip and they came away edged in red. "You think he'll make a break, maybe try to bribe you?"

"Right. And maybe more, especially if I pretend to go along with it."

"I don't like it," she said, shaking a head full of blonde curls.

"What's wrong?"

"It's too contrived. First of all, what made you come up here to scout around for it? Second, how did you know that the K.B. on the clip meant Kingsley Benson? Thirdly, how can you prove he dropped it here last night?"

"Answer one, I came up here to clear myself of the Whipper shooting. Answer two, I recognized the initials because I was the boy who broke the story about K. B. and Karen Lamain being seen together. As for number three, I'll just let his own imagination take care of that. There's no D. A. in the world who can trap a guilty man as well as his own imagination. Now do you buy it?"

She gave ground finally. I knew what was really troubling her. She thought I'd make a slip-up and involve her in the thing. She had a pretty good job, even if it meant working for the slimy soul she described him as. She didn't want to lose the hundred bucks a week. I understood that right off.

"Forget it, honey. My lips are sealed to your name. As far as Benson is concerned, the only Helen I know is the Greek lady whose face launched a navy."

That brought her around, but not without a struggle. We settled that well enough with a couple of kisses. It could have gone past that stage, but there was too much left undone. And there were too many ghosts in that apartment.

CHAPTER FIFTEEN

I drove her downtown in my car and dropped her off at a Fifth Avenue bus stop. Then I drove over to the Benson Tobacco Building on Lexington Avenue and Forty-sixth Street. It was five-fifteen by then. I took a chance on catching the boss man still at his desk.

There was a thin, bespectacled dame with a long nose guarding the entrance to Benson's office. Helen had described her to me as a stork with glasses. I recognized her right off from the description. She was the relief secretary when Helen was out of the office on one of Benson's personal calls.

It took ten minutes of strategic questioning to get the stork-lady to admit that Benson was still in his office. Then she said he was in conference and couldn't be disturbed. Raised voices came filtering through the office door. I recognized one of them as Calvin Stockton's. My luck was getting better by the minute.

I charged past the stork-lady's desk and through a door marked Kingsley Benson, President. She shrieked and plunged after me, grabbing my coattails as I went through the door.

There was a huge modern desk made of some bleached wood. It occupied half of the office. With two hoops it could have been a basketball court. And behind it, big and bald as a watermelon, sat Kingsley Benson.

Calvin Stockton sat in an overstuffed chair in front of the desk. Benson was saying something to him when I came charging in. The sight of a stranger flying through the door with the stork-lady floating from his coattails didn't faze Benson. He went right on to finish his sentence.

"—and if it is possible to settle matters amicably, then by all means let us do so." Then he turned to the stork-lady, glared up the full length of his hawk nose at her and said, "Aren't you a bit old for this sort of thing?"

"This man, he—" she panted. "He—he—he—"

"Stop spluttering and say something," Benson said.

Calvin Stockton stood up, walked in two paces and threw a long right at me. I ducked to the right and the punch whistled past my shoulder with Calvin falling all over me. Then I stepped quickly aside and he fell flat on his face.

I took out a handkerchief and wiped my hands. "Mr. Benson, let me introduce myself. My name is Boyd McGee."

Benson gave out with a loud guffaw and then leaned across the table to shake hands. Calvin stumbled up off the floor in time to catch the friendly gesture.

"But—but Mr. Benson," Calvin stammered. "This is the man who started all the trouble with your wife. This is the—"

"Yes, you damn fool," Benson snarled. "And he's the kind of man I could have done business with in five minutes if I'd had the chance." He turned back to me. "Sit down, Mr. McGee, sit down, And that will be all," he said to the secretary.

The stork-lady took one more look at me and then at Benson, surveyed our smiling faces and then "harrumphed" once and walked out.

Benson opened a humidor of cigars and offered me one. I shook my head and took out a cigarette. He leaned over the desk to give me a light and I studied him above the flame.

His face was lean, hard and dark. The skin had that craggy look that you associate with farmers or merchant seamen. He had an inch-thick sunburn that you don't get from an hour a day on the golf course and his hands were big and raw looking, like they'd never held a pencil in their lives. He was the damnedest-looking business tycoon I ever met.

He lit a long, chocolate-colored cigar, leaned back in his chair and blew a smoke ring. "Now, Mr. McGee, it's time we two got to know each other. I have a public relations department that's supposed to contact newspapermen and build friendly relations with them. And I've got a law firm that's supposed to protect me against the ones who aren't friendly with my P. R. department. But none of that seems to work with you."

I stared down at the tip of my cigarette and rolled it between my fingers. "I didn't come here to discuss that, Mr. Benson. But since you brought it up, I will. You've got a bum named Wheelock running your public relations outfit. He thinks every newsman in town can be bought for two bottles of Scotch and some Paris perfume for the little woman."

"Whereas it takes maybe twice that for some, eh?"

I shook my head at the cigarette. "You don't get it. Most newsmen start out as public crusaders and wind up as private bootlickers. They know that but they don't like being reminded of it. Your man Wheelock is an ex-newsie. That's why he's got no respect for them. He never studied the fine art of seduction. He's strictly a rapist. Get yourself a new man, Mr. Benson. Somebody who can work with a song as well as a sledge hammer."

He smiled and put the cigar in an ashtray. "Are you applying for the job?" I shook my head again. "Wheelock gets three hundred a week. You're worth double that."

"Look, you don't get it, Mr. B. I just offered you some friendly advice. I didn't come in answer to a Help Wanted ad."

He leaned forward in his chair and put both elbows on the desk. "Then what did you come for?"

"To make more trouble," Calvin said. He'd been sulking in the back of the room since he did the nose dive. Now he was coming around to his old sweet self.

"Not to make trouble, Calvin," I said. "To save you some."

"You're doing somebody a favor?" Calvin guffawed. "What's the matter, McGee, did you get a tip that Judgment Day was around the corner?"

"Hold it a minute, Stockton," Benson said. "Let's hear this out." He nodded at me and picked up his cigar again.

"It tells fast," I said. "I caused you a little trouble the other day, Mr. Benson, when—"

"A *little* trouble?" Calvin grumbled. I ignored that and so did Benson.

"—when I ran that item about you and Karen Lamain. Of course, none of that would have happened if Calvin here had leveled with me. I didn't know that you were the client who was being sued for divorce."

Benson turned to Calvin, flicked the cigar over the ashtray and growled, "You bloody fool."

"But, K. B., you expressly said—"

Benson turned his back on Calvin. I went on with it. "So it wasn't exactly my fault about that item but I felt a little responsible. That's why I came here, to make it up to you."

"How?" Benson asked. Calvin was muttering some dire warnings in the background but Benson was all with me now. I'd sold him a bill of goods.

"Mr. Benson, I know that your relations with Karen Lamain were strictly business. I also know what that business was."

"You see?" Calvin howled. "He's with her. He's been on her side from the start." By her, Calvin meant Mrs. Benson, not Karen Lamain. Calvin figured I was working for the Reno lady.

"Shut up," Benson said. Calvin shut up.

I started working up a righteous anger. "I don't know your wife, Mr. Benson. I wouldn't know her if I banged into her on the street. I'm not on anybody's side in this." I got up to go. "I just wanted to do a favor for a man I may have wronged. I can see now that you don't need my help." I started for the door.

"Stop him, Calvin," Benson shouted. "Stop him or that doddering law firm of yours will lose its biggest account. I mean that." He did, too.

Calvin raced me to the door. I let him win it. "McGee, please listen to reason."

I brought up my hands and examined my nails. "Please," Calvin said. "Listen to reason. If I've said anything in the past that—that may have—that you might have—" He couldn't get on with it. When you're born in a silver cradle, educated by private tutors and led by the hand through Harvard Law School with three hundred a week for beer and Kleenex, apologies just stick in your throat.

I put one arm around his shoulder and looked him deep in his baby blues. "That's all right, Calvin. I understand."

He smiled and batted back the tears. "Good of you, McGee. Really good of you." I turned walked over to Benson's desk and sat on one corner of it; it was probably the first time such a posture had ever been taken in front of this mogul.

"Let me show you how well I understand," I said. "Benson, you needed a cagey dame who could trick your wife into breaking her divorce residence. Calvin here quietly contacted a divorce lawyer who knew just such a woman— one who had done that kind of job for him before—Karen Lamain. She must have needed the money or she would never have come out of hiding to do jobs like that.... I don't say this is how it went line for line. But I'll bet my last Chiclet that it's damn close."

Benson said nothing. I was close, all right. "But Karen decided to double-cross you and warn Mrs. Benson away before you and your witnesses could catch her in town. You got wind of that and broke into the Lamain apartment at the time originally set for your meeting with Mrs. Benson."

"You're out of your mind, McGee," Calvin shouted.

Benson sighed. "Shut up, Calvin," he said. "Let him finish."

"That's it. Charlie Whipper broke jail that same night and was shot to death in the Lamain elevator. If the police learned that you were present they might think—" I shrugged my shoulders. I wasn't sure what the cops would think. So I just let Benson imagine the rest.

He didn't seem troubled by the idea. He practically laughed in my face. "I suppose you've got some proof that I was present in the Lamain apartment that night, McGee?" I decided to wipe the smile off his face. "As a matter of fact, I have. You see, you dropped something on your way out. A very important something. A money clip with your initials on it. Of course I didn't bring the clip with me, but—"

He was laughing now. Something had gone completely haywire. I shot a quick glance at Calvin. The lawyer stood confused for one moment. Then he began laughing too.

"It's funny?" I asked. "Well, maybe the cops won't laugh as hard."

Benson went on laughing. He pulled a handkerchief from his pocket and wiped tears from his eyes. Then, between chuckles, he threw open a desk drawer and pulled out something and chucked it on the desk. He stifled the laughter for one moment. "Is this what you found, Mr. McGee? Is this the evidence that will send me to the chair?" He burst into loud laughter again. On his desk was a solid silver money clip with his initials.

If I had to do it again, I'd make the same play. Nine times out of ten it will work. The only trouble was that Benson didn't drop his money clip in the Lamain apartment. Wherever he misplaced it he'd found it again. And there I stood with my bare lie hanging out.

In cases like that the best offense is a good defense. So I put my tail between my legs and beat a hasty retreat. The funny thing was that when I'd walked into that office I wasn't convinced that Benson had put the slug on Whipper. I went there to try and trick him into convicting himself. The trick didn't work. But even so, there was something about him, his loud laughter, his bold self-confidence in the face of disaster, his shrewd sense of timing—something that convinced me that Benson was my man.

They were still laughing when I stumbled out the door and slammed it behind me. But I remembered Mr. Aesop's saying about he who laughs last. I had a couple of ha-ha's coming to me pretty soon—laughs that Benson wouldn't enjoy.

I went outside and headed for my car. Along the way I stopped in at a drug store to call Doctor Ervin. He'd been waiting past his workday for my call.

"You're in a bad position, Mr. McGee," he said.

"How's that?"

"We sent Miss Page home about an hour ago. But

before that I had a chat with her. That girl is in love with you."

I smiled into the phone. "I forgot to tell you about that," I said. "Maura's in love with lots of guys. Practically everyone she meets."

"Nymphomaniac?"

"Something like that, I guess."

"Hmmm, that changes things a bit. However, unless I'm mistaken, her feeling for you is stronger than that. And unless I'm mistaken again, your feeling for her is—"

"Look, I've got maybe fifteen years on her, Doc. That's more like a father than a lover."

"Well, that's for you to decide. For you and *her*. But either way, as of this moment that young lady is very dependent upon you. You've got to help her along. You mustn't make her think that her love is being betrayed. With your help she could regain complete health far more quickly."

"And without it?" I asked.

"That's not for me to judge, at the moment."

"Mmm. I understand, Doc. We better have another talk sometime soon."

"Just so. Call my office soon and arrange for it."

"I'll be in touch with you, Doctor Ervin."

"Yes, and—uh—good luck, Mr. McGee."

I hung up and walked back to the car. I decided to give Maura a ring as soon as I got home. I figured I might take her around to the clubs with me while I worked up a column. I didn't like to think of her sitting alone in that room with the Mexican paintings. The thought pressed on me like the downstroke of a giant piston. I didn't know why.

I drove home at a slow pace, thinking things out. I

wanted to do what I could for the kid without bending my own life out of shape. Her folks were about as helpful to her as meningitis. And a kid like Maura didn't specialize in collecting friends. That left me. I could almost feel the halo floating slowly down upon my head as I pulled the car up to my doorway. There was only one small thing bothering me. Dr. Ervin had hinted at it. The question was, was I falling for the kid with the haunted eyes and the hot pants?

There were cops all over the place, on the sidewalk, across the street, in the lobby of the building. Somebody had probably lost a Mickey Mouse watch or a silver toothpick. I brushed past the Johns and walked into the elevator. Joe, the operator, shut the door and we started upstairs.

"Geeze, Mr. McGee, I'm glad you got here. You should have seen the—"

"Don't tell me about cops, Joe. I don't want to hear about cops or detectives or flatfoots again for the rest of my life—if not later."

"Yeah, but—" He brought the elevator to a stop.

"But me no buts, Joe. Just let me crawl onto my bed for a few minutes. I've still got to make the rounds tonight and I'm not feeling exactly joyous about it." He opened the elevator door and I exited.

The hall was like a scene out of Dante's Inferno. Newspapermen, photographers, cops, stretcher bearers, all shouting and milling around. Fallon was there. The freckle-faced lieutenant was running up and down, barking orders and looking worried. And in the background, trying to stay under cover, was Lieutenant Governor Colombo and the two scrub-heads.

Fallon spotted me and came over wearing a face-wide smile. "Well, that does it, McGee. That idea of luring her down here with your column did the trick. You're a genius, man."

"Yeah," I whispered. I stared dumbly at the crowd massed near the door of my apartment. "Yeah, a real genius. Only would you mind telling me what in hell happened?"

"You mean you don't know we got the Lamain dame?"

"Here? She showed here?" He nodded and started talking. But I wasn't listening. I was thinking. I didn't have to make the rounds that night. Karen Lamain in custody meant I could use the whole story for the next day's column. And maybe for more than that.

"—we had a general alarm out," Fallon was saying. "But the boys couldn't pick her up. No wonder. She was wearing weeds—widow's weeds."

I smiled. "Mourning for dear old Charlie?"

The freckle-faced lieutenant broke in. "Mourning, hell. With that black veil and a dress shaped like a bag she could have been your grandmother. She was hiding out in black. I had two guys covering the building front and back. How the hell was I to know she'd enter by another building and climb over the roof?"

Fallon glared at him. "We'll talk about that later, *officer*." There's only one time when you call a lieutenant "officer"—that's when he's an ex-lieutenant. That's what Fallon was planning for Freckles.

"Great," I said. "So justice triumphed in the end, Fallon. Don't tell me the whole story, let me read it in the comic books. Just tell me about the money. Has she talked yet?"

He frowned with his bushy eyebrows. "You never heard a word I said, McGee. Talk, hell. She's dead!"

CHAPTER SIXTEEN

A woman screamed from the center of the mob. "Let me be. I don't know anything. I found her that way. Please let me be. Please, please."

I recognized the voice and pushed through the crowd. It was Maura. There were four cops and six reporters surrounding her. She wore a skirt and sweater two sizes too big for her. They must have belonged to Doctor Ervin's nurse. Flashbulbs popped everywhere. She winced with each one. The whole stinking business was guaranteed to send her permanently off her rocker.... She saw me then and rushed into my arms. One of the Johns tried to pull her off. I showed him the back of my hand. "Let her alone, cop!" Another flash bulb went off. It made a pretty picture.

"Boyd," she moaned. "Boyd, make them stop."

"Sure," I said. "Sure, baby, sure."

"I came to see you. I came from the doctor's. I wanted to show you how much better I was. I thought you'd be proud of me."

"I am, baby." I stroked her hair. "I'm real proud."

"Then I found her." She pointed back without looking. It was toward the door of my apartment. The white-jackets were loading the body of a woman onto their stretcher. A black hat and veil toppled from her head. Her face was a cold, white, beautiful stone set in a crown of blue-black hair. As they moved her the black skirt fell past her thighs. Her legs were long and shapely, not skinny. Her breasts rose in twin peaks, between them a dark splotch of blood and burned cloth. She'd been shot at close range.

I held Maura against me while they carried the body away. The elevator opened and a cop came out as the stretcher boys went in. The cop approached Fallon and whispered something. Fallon nodded and came over to me. Maura buried her head deeper in the pocket of my shoulder.

"That tears it," Fallon said. "We've just been talking to this Dr. Ervin. The doc tells us that Maura here has quite a crush on you. Yeah, quite a crush."

She pulled her head from my shoulder. "Stop it," she hissed. "You're filthy—filthy—filthy."

I pressed her head back and ran my hand over her hair. "So what?" I said to Fallon.

"She was standing like that over the Lamain woman when the elevator man got here. She claims the woman was dead. We claim she shot her. Motive, jealousy—crazy, raving jealousy. Dr. Ervin just gave us that."

I closed my eyes for one moment. The whole thing made a weird kind of sense. But I tried to fight it anyway. "The gun? What about that?"

"It was lying beside the body. We haven't had time to get a report on prints. For crying out loud, McGee, we just got here five minutes ago."

"You don't get the girl until the prints come through," I said. I put both arms around her then.

"Look," Fallon said. "Be sensible. We're not trying to frame the girl. She's out of her mind. She just walked out of a nut doctor's office. They'll never convict her."

There was that much on her side. Pleading insanity isn't a happy business. But you'll take the best deal you can get when you're fighting for your life.

"What do you say?" Fallon asked.

Maura looked at me, tears staining her cheeks. "No,"

she pleaded. "Don't let them take me away, Boyd. Tell them I didn't do it. Tell them...."

I wanted to. More than anything else I wanted to tell them she didn't do it. But I couldn't. Fallon's logic was too sharp, too complete. The girl had just walked out of a nerve specialist's office to see a man she thought she loved. On the doorstep of his home she finds another woman, a pretty woman. Her mind snaps completely and she murders the other woman in one dark, wild moment. It made too much sense to fight it.

"Well?" Fallon repeated. "Do we take her quietly or do we just take her?" He pointed his thumb at Maura and three uniformed cops moved toward us. That would have been the worst that could happen—if we'd fought then and there over her physically, throwing fists and feet. The shock would have been more than she could bear. I could have made a show of it. It wouldn't have cost me more than a black eye and a few lumps. But it might have cost her much more—a life of complete insanity.

I gave her up. It wasn't easy. She was crying and tearing at me when they pulled her off. I was sick down in the pit of my stomach.

Lieutenant Governor Colombo and the scrub-heads waited till the newspaper boys had followed the cops downstairs. They were practically the last to go. They came over to congratulate me while one of the building workers scrubbed some blood from the carpet in front of my door. I told the lieutenant governor, as politely as I knew how, to drop dead.

I went into the apartment and lay down on the couch. The street was dark now except for a couple of lamplights. I didn't bother turning on the light in the room. One yellow street light filtered through my window and cast filmy shadows upon the wall.

I lay there for an hour or more, staring up at the wall and thinking about nothing and everything. My mind couldn't light on anything long enough to make sense out of it. I felt all burned out inside of me.

I couldn't write a column about Karen Lamain and Charlie Whipper and Sam and the rest of it. I couldn't do anything until I'd heard from Fallon. If they got the reports back from ballistics and fingerprints and if they decided to charge Maura with the killing, I knew I'd never write that column.

So there was nothing to do but get up and start out on the night's rounds. Your brain may fold up and your heart can sink into a sea of darkness, but those damn presses keep rolling and they keep on eating up words. And you'll keep on feeding them or you'll look for another job.

I got up and washed around the face and neck and ran a quick razor around the blue shadow on my chin. I put on a clean shirt and climbed back into the same jacket I'd worn during the day. The doorbell rang.

It was Helen Brooks. Suddenly I didn't mind a little company. I threw on some lights, invited her in and poured us both a drink. She took she shoes off and climbed into that Buddha position of hers.

I told her about Karen Lamain's death and about the cops taking Maura downtown. She sympathized with me and I poured another drink. Then I told her about Benson and the money clip. She laughed and then she cursed him once or twice. But she reminded me that she herself had warned me about him. He was a cool man. I admitted she was right and poured us another drink.

It was beginning to get kind of warm then. I took off my jacket and threw it on a chair. My gun clunked out and I chucked that back on that chair.

We sat around talking about Benson and Karen Lamain and Charlie Whipper. Whipper's death was the only thing left unaccounted for—that and the blackmail money. We talked that over. Helen had her head propped on my shoulder and she fed us both whiskey from the same glass.

"There's something missing, Boyd," she said.

"Soda," I said. "Or maybe ginger ale?"

She laughed. "No, not the whiskey. I like mine neat, like this. No, I mean there's something missing from this whole business. Some clue or piece of evidence that would throw it all into perspective."

"Perspective," I said. "That's a good word." The drinks were big and I was beginning to feel them.

"Yes," she said. "For instance, Maura Page shot this Lamain woman on your doorstep."

"So they say."

"So they say," she repeated. "But what was Karen Lamain doing here to begin with?" I started to answer but she took the words out of my mouth. "Coming in answer to the line in your column?" I nodded, yes. She shook her head, no. I bit her on the ear. She laughed.

"I don't think so," she continued. "I think there was something stronger pulling her here. Boyd, are you sure you didn't pick up something at her house, something of real value to a woman like her?"

"You mean some of her stock? Like some blackmail letters or some photographs or—"

"Yes," she said, her eyes twinkling into mine. "Or some film negatives or wire recordings or—well, anything that she could use to raise some cash?"

"Not a chance, honey," I said. "All I did was look the place over once or twice. I saw some stuff there, microphones and so forth. But I didn't touch any of it. There's no chance that she came to get something from me. Of course she might have planted the stuff here for safekeeping while I was out on the job." I laughed. "But that would be a damn fool thing to do." I leaned forward to pick up the whiskey bottle again when I suddenly remembered something. My hand froze in mid-air.

"The noose!" I said.

"The what?" she said.

"The wire noose." I jumped up and grabbed my jacket off the chair. The wire noose was still there in the pocket. I yanked it out and held it up in the air. "It wasn't from Kincaid. I should have known he wasn't a man for subtleties. If he wanted to send me a drop-dead letter, he'd have done it with plain, hard words. Not gimmicks."

"I don't—" she said.

"Don't you see, honey? You put me on the right track. This piece of wire—it's a recording. The knot was here just to hold the pieces of wire together. I suppose there was a break in the recording and she knotted them together like this." I held up the noose.

"Then that's what she was after?"

"Exactly. This is the blackmail evidence that Whipper used against the governor. They told me he used personal witnesses. But Whipper was too smart for that. Witnesses can be bought, sold and killed. But a little piece of wire like this—" I held it up and kissed the steel noose. "This it, by God."

"I—I suppose you're right," she said. "Only it's all so—so—" The phone rang.

"So wonderful," I said. "That's what it is."

I headed for the phone. "We know what the noose is now. All we've got to do is get in on a recording machine. That piece of wire might just save Maura's life. It might just prove that somebody else killed Karen Lamain. Maybe the governor himself, by God."

I picked up the phone and sang a cheery hello into it. "McGee," a voice answered, "this is Kingsley Benson."

"Hello, you old bald-headed bat."

"You're unusually chipper considering our meeting this afternoon. I thought you'd be rather angry at me."

"Why?" I asked. "Just because you made a damn fool out of me? Hell, that happens every day."

"Well, that's neither here nor there," he said. "I've been sitting at home thinking about that conversation we had, especially that part about the money clip. Who told you about that?"

"What difference does that make?" I asked. I wanted to get rid of him. Helen was beginning to stir around in the living room.

"Just this," he said. "My wife gave me that five years ago when we became engaged. I hated it from the first moment, it was so large and gaudy. She has terrible taste, Mrs. Benson."

Helen called in from the living room. "Oh, hang up, Boyd. You're spoiling the party."

"Yeah, yeah," I said to both Helen and the phone.

"So I've never used that clip from that day to this. I kept it stuck away in my desk drawer. No one but myself, my wife and Helen Brooks ever knew it existed."

"Uh-huh," I said.

"You know Miss Brooks," he said. "She's my secretary.

The tall, thin lady with the rather large nose who tried to keep you from—"

"She's what?" I gasped. Then there was another voice in the room.

"Who's on the phone?" she asked. She had a gun in her hand now. My gun.

"So you see," Benson's voice crackled, "the only one who could have told you about that clip is my wife."

"Who is it?" she repeated. "My darling husband?" I nodded my head. "All right, just hang up the phone very quietly."

I hung up. "Now step back into the living room," she said.

"You're not Helen Brooks," I said, "Mrs. Benson."

She laughed. "Darling, how did you ever guess?"

"Just sheer genius," I said. "Sheer, stupid genius."

She laughed again and motioned me back into the living room. I followed her instructions. That gun was loaded and it had already killed one man that day.

I sat down on the couch. She picked up the steel noose. "This knot, Boyd dear, it's not there because the wire was broken. It's there because these are two separate recordings. One is something to do with the governor. You'd know more about that than I. But the other—"

"No," I said. "Allow me. Maybe I can prove how stupid a genius I really am.... The other recording was made about ten o'clock last night in Karen Lamain's apartment. It was a record of your interview with Karen during which she told you how your husband, Benson, was trapping you into breaking your Reno residence requirement."

"Exactly," Mrs. Benson said. "She was selling me the privilege of escaping that for five thousand dollars.

Cheap at twice the price, if she kept her word."

"But you had reason to believe she wouldn't keep her word, right?"

"I'm not as big a fool as my husband. I know that when you do business with people like that you can't turn your back for a minute. I gave her my notarized check for five thousand dollars and I left the apartment. But I remained in the hall, listening at her door."

"And you heard voices, eh? Two of them, Karen and Charlie Whipper, right?"

"Yes. Obviously he had broken out of jail and barged right in on the situation. But nevertheless he was prepared to take advantage of it. By listening at the door I learned that Whipper had been hiding in the apartment all the time I was there, recording everything I said. You see, he was preparing to pull one more job—one grand coup."

"Yeah," I said. "A brilliant one, too. He was going to pull a *triple-cross*. First Karen makes a deal with Benson to trap you. Then she makes a deal with you to double-cross Benson. And finally, hubby Charlie records that deal so he can sell it to Benson. With that recording Benson could have proved to the court that your legal residence was falsified."

"Exactly," she said. She picked her purse up from the chair without taking her eyes from me or lowering the gun. "I heard all that in the hallway. Then I just waited on the stairs until Whipper left the apartment. He took the elevator and I ran down the stairs. I beat him to the first floor, opened the elevator door and shot him. I searched the body and found my notarized check. But the recording wasn't there."

"Of course not," I said. "Karen had it. She took it

with her after you shot Charlie and she mailed it to me when the heat was on her. That's what she came here for."

"I was waiting across the street," she said. She opened her purse and dropped the wire recording inside, still keeping her eyes and the gun fixed on me. "I was afraid that you might have learned too much when you went to see my husband."

"You mean you came to kill me, not Karen Lamain?"

She smiled. "Possibly. I didn't want it to come to that but—" She shrugged.

"Instead you spotted Karen and followed her up to my place. You used the gun on her, searched her and then slipped back down the stairs."

"I did. But it was useless. The recording wasn't on her either."

"You must have been ready to flip your top."

She smiled again. "Not at all. I knew where it was then. I knew that you must have had it without realizing it. I knew what I had to do then." She started backing out of the room. I heard a click. It was the safety being released. All the while I was praying she wouldn't know about that. But she did, the doll.

"Look, Mrs. Benson, let's talk this over."

"No time," she said. "I don't like doing this. You're the nicest man I've met in a long while. If I could have won that million dollars from Benson, you and I could have had some good times together."

"We still could," I said. Her shoes were on the floor just behind her. I figured maybe she'd trip over them. She didn't. But she didn't know that. "Look out!" I yelled. "Your shoes—you'll trip over them!"

She looked down quickly at the floor. I jumped five feet forward from a sitting position. It must have been some kind of record. I landed around her waist and threw her to the ground.

She rolled out from under me. I grabbed the collar of her dress and she pulled away. There was a loud rip and the dress came away in my hands. But she was free and the gun looked right down at me.

I clubbed up at her gun hand and there was a shot. The gun fell and she went down with it. It wasn't a bad wound, an inch below the left shoulder, but blood flowed down her chest, into her brassiere and between her breasts.

I picked up the gun and went out to the phone. I started dialing the cops, but there was a loud banging at my door before I could finish. The door opened and Joe, the elevator boy, let Captain Fallon and some cops into the apartment.

"You all right, McGee?" Fallon yelled.

"Yeah, just fine," I said. "Never been better."

"We got a call from Kingsley Benson saying he thought his wife was up here when he called you. She's supposed to be a dangerous—" He walked into the living room and whistled. "Not anymore she isn't." He shook his head. "McGee, if you've got any more bodies lying around here will you drag them out now and get it over with?"

I chucked my gun on the floor. "No more, Captain. She accounts for Whipper's death and Karen Lamain as well. But if you don't open that cell and let Maura Page out before midnight, I might have to pick up that gun again."

She was out by nine o'clock. I took her home and we had a long talk. We've had a lot more since then. She doesn't think she's in love with all the boys anymore.

I cured her of that without Dr. Ervin's help. What she needed most was somebody to tell it all to, little by little. And all I needed was a good night's sleep. She lets me get that now and then.

About the dough, we never found that. But I've got a theory that might account for it. When Whipper wrote his wife from jail she used a blind post office box number to cover her real address. I think Karen used the same gimmick to hide the money when she took off the night Charlie was killed. I think she stuck it in a plain brown wrapper, addressed it to herself care of some general post office in some town in one of the forty-eight states and then dropped it into a mailbox.

That means the package will lie around in the office for a while, waiting for a dead woman to collect it. After that it goes into one of those general auctions as a blind item. So if you want to pick up a half million in cash the easy way, just drop down to the nearest post office around auction time and buy up every plain, brown wrapper package they put up for sale. You might make it.

THE END

Arnold Jack Drake was born March 1, 1924, in New York City. At age 12 he contracted scarlet fever, and while confined to bed he began drawing his own comics. Years later he studied journalism and turned his career toward writing, collaborating with Leslie Waller (as Drake Waller) and artist Matt Baker to create the proto-graphic novel, *It Rhymes With Lust*, in 1950. After meeting Batman creator Bob Kane, who introduced Drake to the editors at DC Comics, he went on to write for them, co-creating Deadman and the Doom Patrol, and the Marvel Comics characters the Guardians of the Galaxy. He also wrote two movie screenplays (*The Flesh Eaters* and *Who Killed Teddy Bear*), as well as lyrics for musicals. In 2005, Drake received the first annual Bill Finger Award for Excellence in Comics Writing. And after his death from pneumonia on March 12, 2007, Drake was posthumously inducted into the Will Eisner Comic Book Hall of Fame in 2008.

www.ingramcontent.com/pod-product-compliance
Lightning Source LLC
Chambersburg PA
CBHW050337160726
48002CB00001B/350

* 9 7 9 8 8 8 6 0 1 0 9 2 3 *